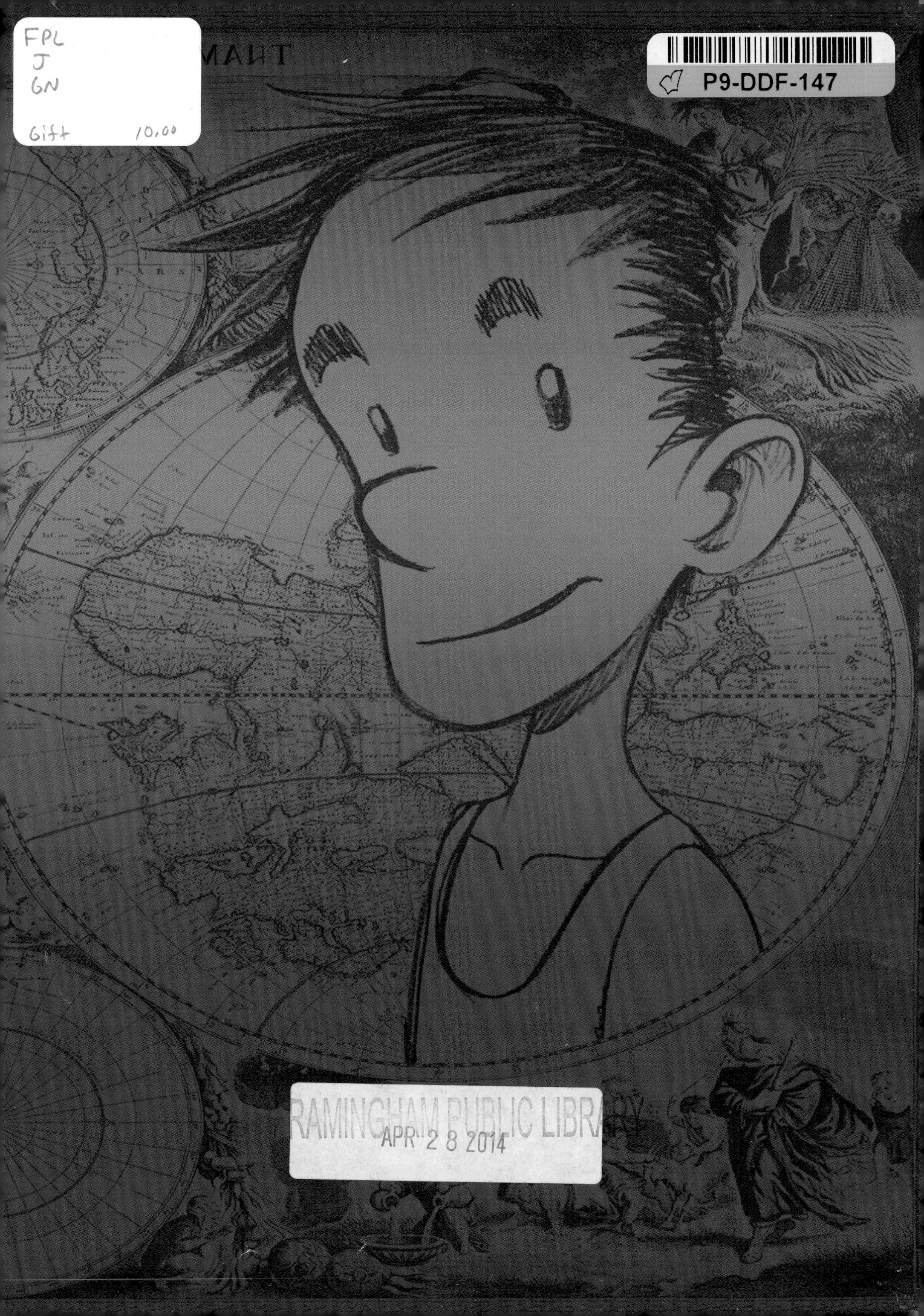

the ElseWhere Chronicles

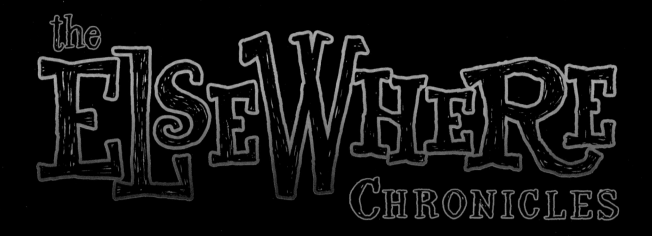

BOOK SIX
THE TOWER OF SHADOWS

Suny Cola

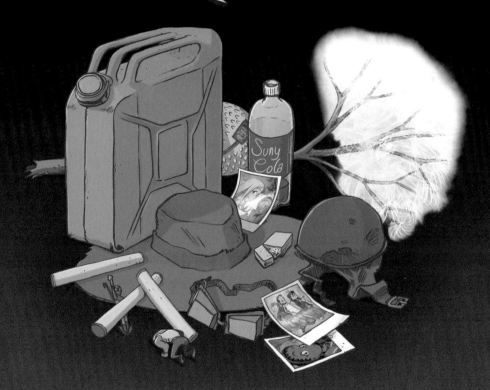

ART
BANNISTER

STORY
NYKKO

COLORS
JAFFRÉ

GRAPHIC UNIVERSE™ · MINNEAPOLIS

Previously . . .

By chance, Rebecca, Max, Theo, and Noah discover a passageway to another world. Trapped on the other side, they work together to travel across dangerous lands haunted by ghostlike creatures that are controlled by a sinister character called the Master of Shadows. After the death of Ilvanna, they will not come out of this fantastic adventure unscathed.

Rebecca is struck by an incurable illness from the Other World and has to go back there, with the ghost of Ilvanna as her guide. With the help of Noah, Theo, and Max, Rebecca meets Gabe, the grandfather she thought was dead and buried. He is a cantankerous old man who seems to know the secrets of this Other World. Profoundly shaken up by the tragic disappearance of Noah, Rebecca and her friends must continue their long journey to confront the Master of Shadows.

Thank you to Carol Burrell for her
help and her work on all six books.
—BAnnister

To Andrée, so that who she was does
not disappear into the Shadows...
For Sabine, Léo and Noé.
—Nykko

To Mathilde and my parents.
—Jaffré

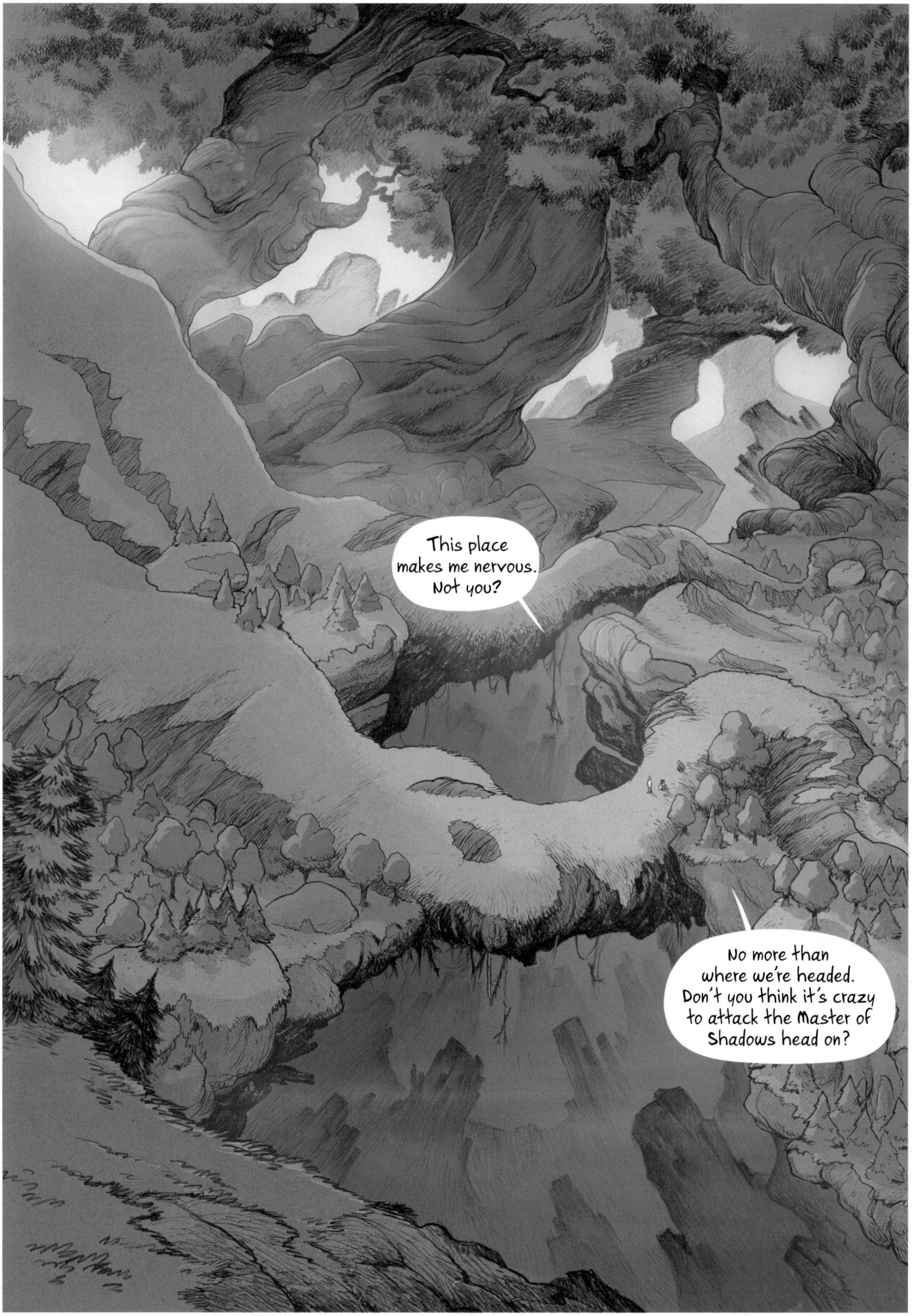
This place makes me nervous. Not you?
No more than where we're headed. Don't you think it's crazy to attack the Master of Shadows head on?

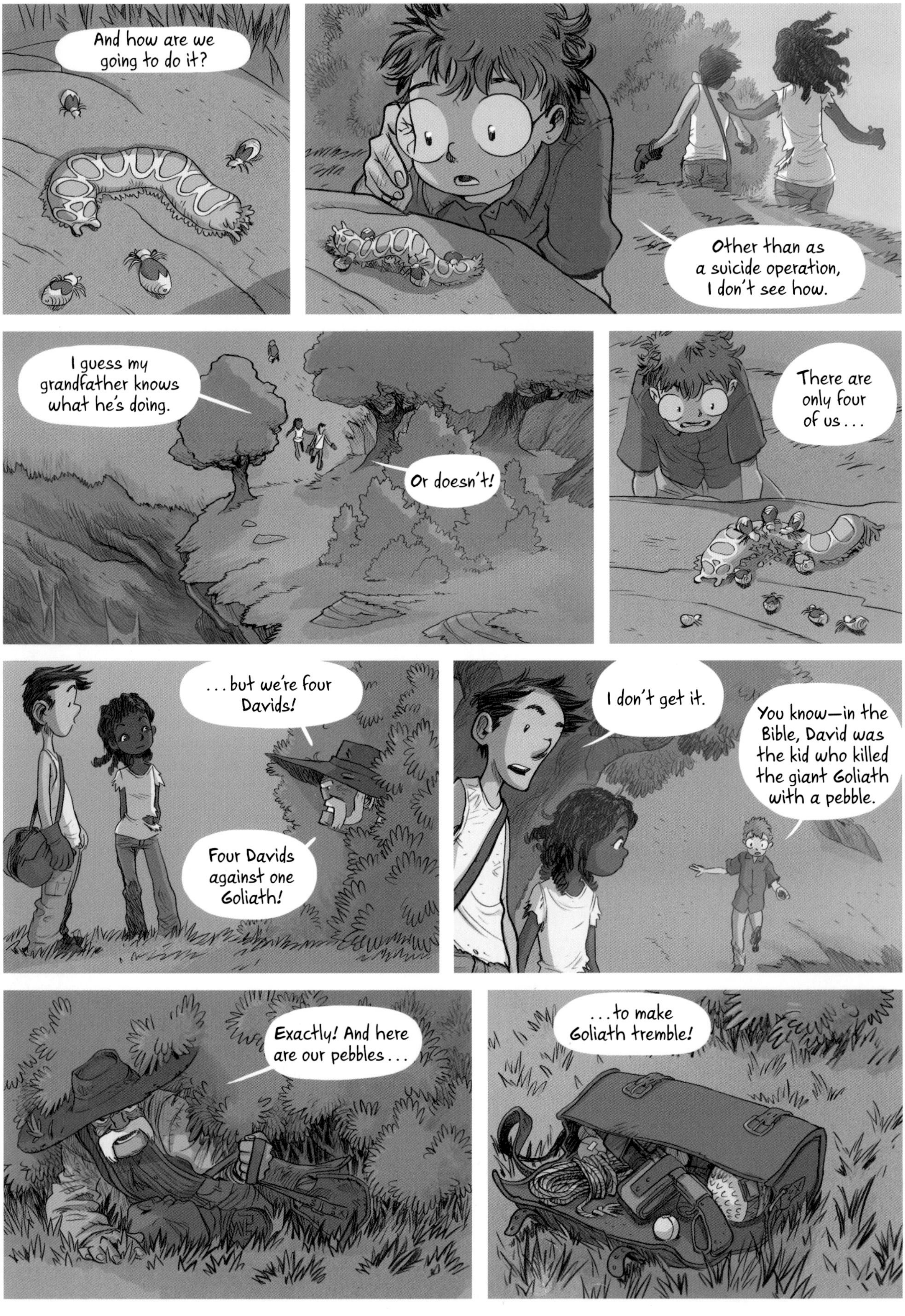
And how are we going to do it?
Other than as a suicide operation, I don't see how.
I guess my grandfather knows what he's doing.
Or doesn't!
There are only four of us . . .
. . . but we're four Davids!
Four Davids against one Goliath!
I don't get it.
You know—in the Bible, David was the kid who killed the giant Goliath with a pebble.
Exactly! And here are our pebbles . . .
. . . to make Goliath tremble!

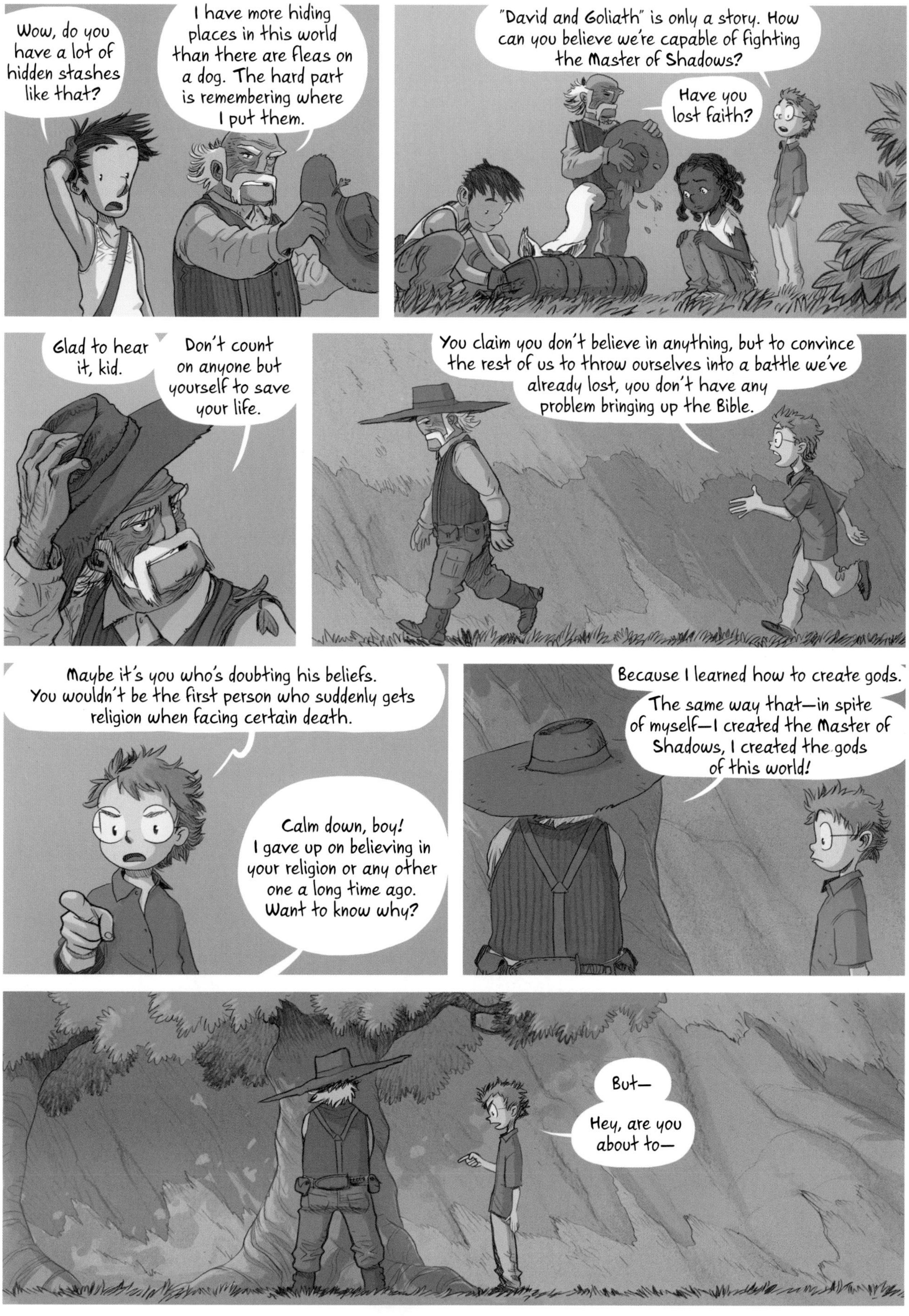
Wow, do you have a lot of hidden stashes like that?
I have more hiding places in this world than there are fleas on a dog. The hard part is remembering where I put them.
"David and Goliath" is only a story. How can you believe we're capable of fighting the Master of Shadows?
Have you lost faith?
Glad to hear it, kid.
Don't count on anyone but yourself to save your life.
You claim you don't believe in anything, but to convince the rest of us to throw ourselves into a battle we've already lost, you don't have any problem bringing up the Bible.
Maybe it's you who's doubting his beliefs. You wouldn't be the first person who suddenly gets religion when facing certain death.
Calm down, boy! I gave up on believing in your religion or any other one a long time ago. Want to know why?
Because I learned how to create gods.
The same way that—in spite of myself—I created the Master of Shadows, I created the gods of this world!
But—
Hey, are you about to—

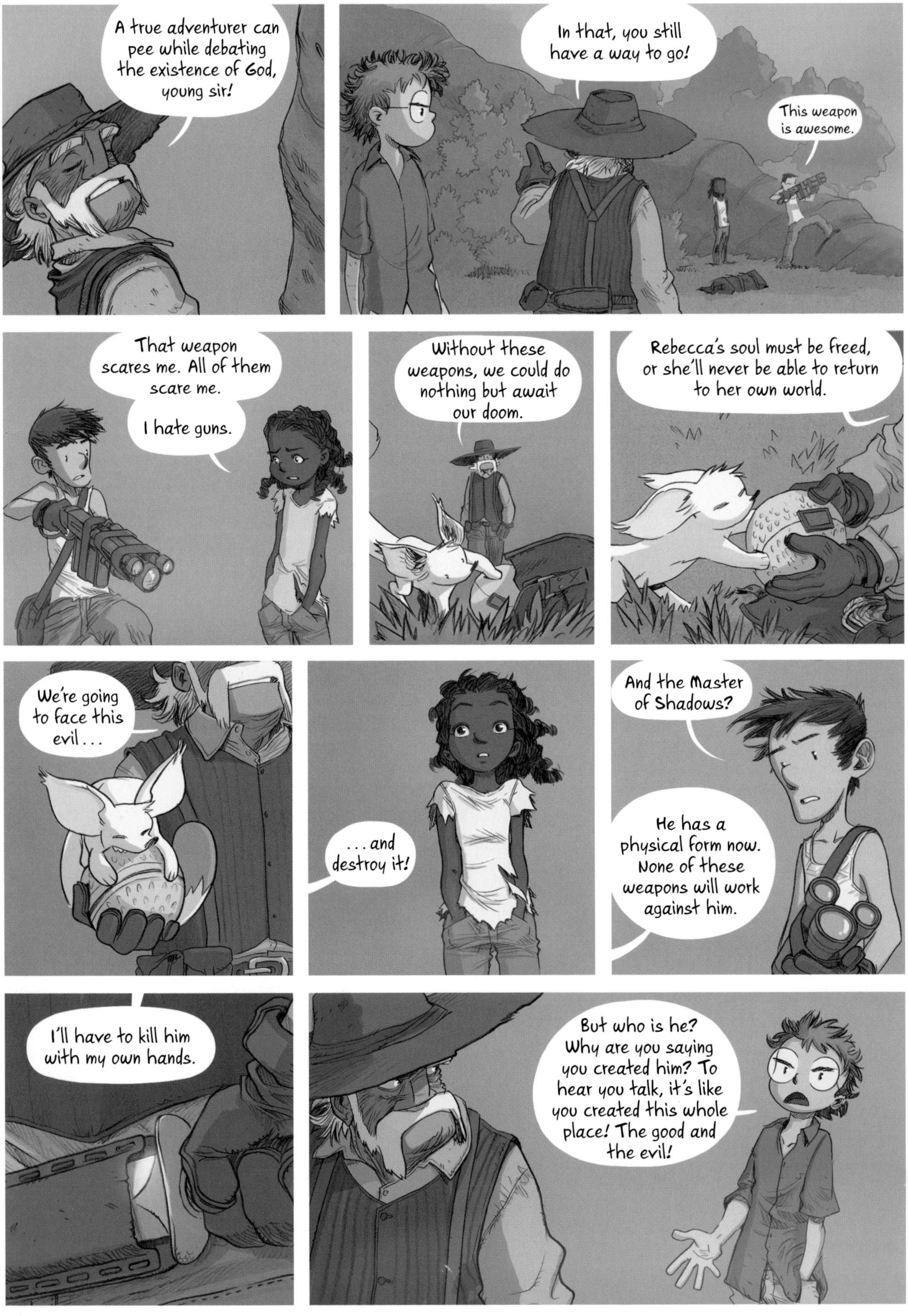
A true adventurer can pee while debating the existence of God, young sir!
In that, you still have a way to go!
This weapon is awesome.
That weapon scares me. All of them scare me.
I hate guns.
Without these weapons, we could do nothing but await our doom.
Rebecca's soul must be freed, or she'll never be able to return to her own world.
We're going to face this evil...
...and destroy it!
And the Master of Shadows?
He has a physical form now. None of these weapons will work against him.
I'll have to kill him with my own hands.
But who is he? Why are you saying you created him? To hear you talk, it's like you created this whole place! The good and the evil!

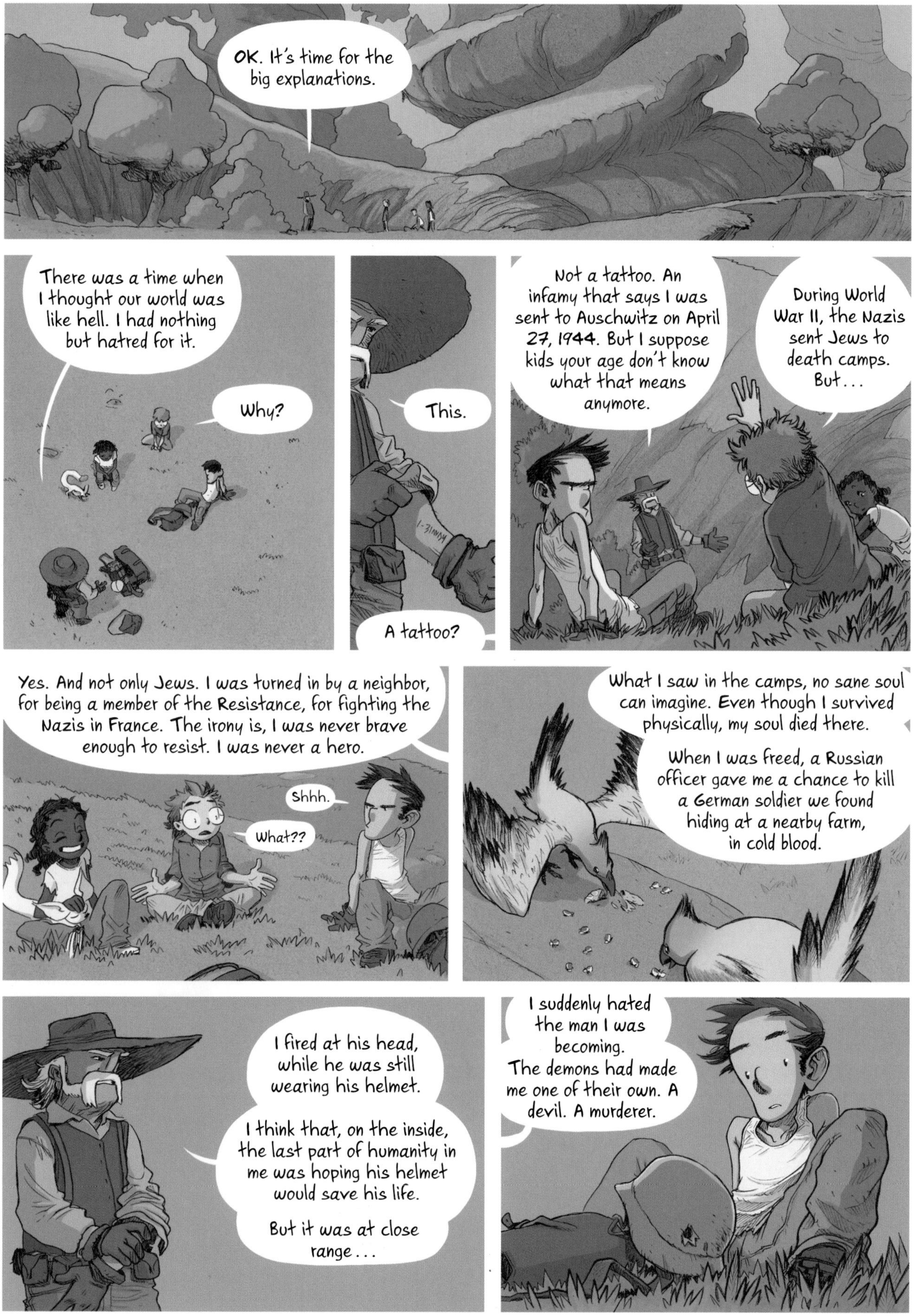
OK. It's time for the big explanations.
There was a time when I thought our world was like hell. I had nothing but hatred for it.
Why?
This.
A tattoo?
Not a tattoo. An infamy that says I was sent to Auschwitz on April 27, 1944. But I suppose kids your age don't know what that means anymore.
During World War II, the Nazis sent Jews to death camps. But . . .
Yes. And not only Jews. I was turned in by a neighbor, for being a member of the Resistance, for fighting the Nazis in France. The irony is, I was never brave enough to resist. I was never a hero.
Shhh.
What??
What I saw in the camps, no sane soul can imagine. Even though I survived physically, my soul died there.
When I was freed, a Russian officer gave me a chance to kill a German soldier we found hiding at a nearby farm, in cold blood.
I fired at his head, while he was still wearing his helmet.
I think that, on the inside, the last part of humanity in me was hoping his helmet would save his life.
But it was at close range . . .
I suddenly hated the man I was becoming. The demons had made me one of their own. A devil. A murderer.

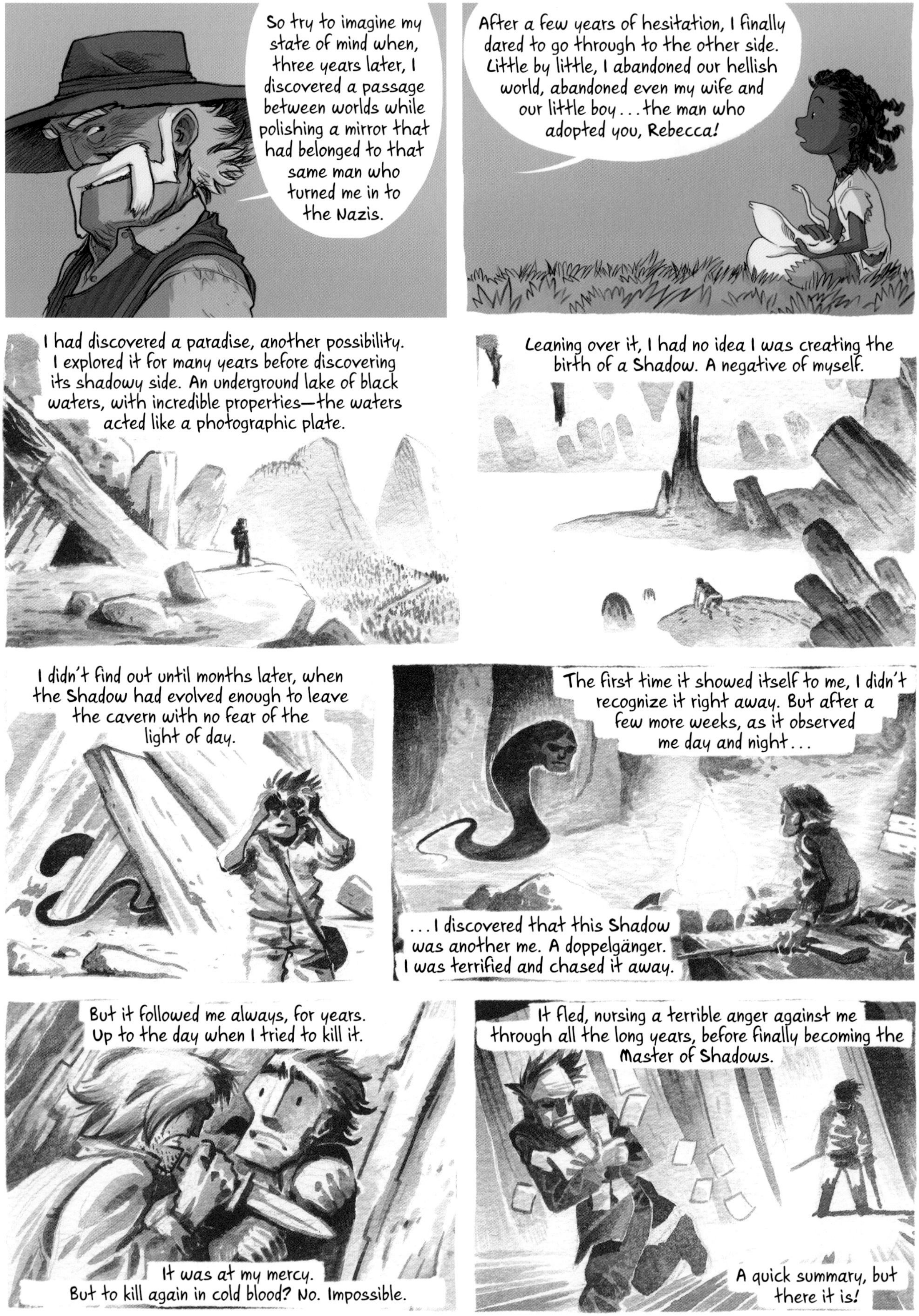
So try to imagine my state of mind when, three years later, I discovered a passage between worlds while polishing a mirror that had belonged to that same man who turned me in to the Nazis.
After a few years of hesitation, I finally dared to go through to the other side. Little by little, I abandoned our hellish world, abandoned even my wife and our little boy . . . the man who adopted you, Rebecca!
I had discovered a paradise, another possibility. I explored it for many years before discovering its shadowy side. An underground lake of black waters, with incredible properties—the waters acted like a photographic plate.
Leaning over it, I had no idea I was creating the birth of a Shadow. A negative of myself.
I didn't find out until months later, when the Shadow had evolved enough to leave the cavern with no fear of the light of day.
The first time it showed itself to me, I didn't recognize it right away. But after a few more weeks, as it observed me day and night . . .
. . . I discovered that this Shadow was another me. A doppelgänger. I was terrified and chased it away.
But it followed me always, for years. Up to the day when I tried to kill it.
It was at my mercy. But to kill again in cold blood? No. Impossible.
It fled, nursing a terrible anger against me through all the long years, before finally becoming the Master of Shadows.
A quick summary, but there it is!

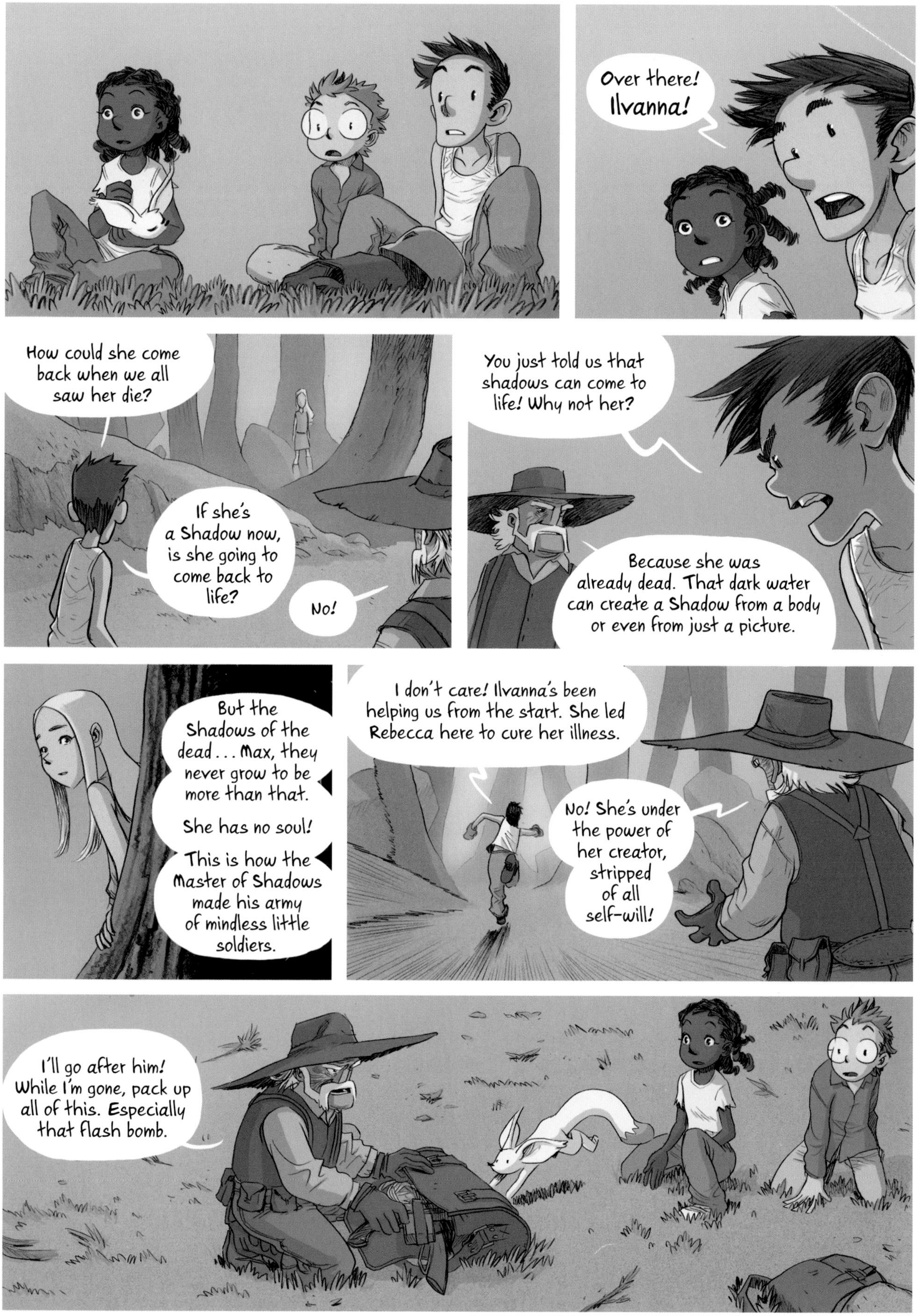
Over there! Ilvanna!
How could she come back when we all saw her die?
You just told us that shadows can come to life! Why not her?
If she's a Shadow now, is she going to come back to life?
No!
Because she was already dead. That dark water can create a Shadow from a body or even from just a picture.
But the Shadows of the dead . . . Max, they never grow to be more than that.
She has no soul!
This is how the Master of Shadows made his army of mindless little soldiers.
I don't care! Ilvanna's been helping us from the start. She led Rebecca here to cure her illness.
No! She's under the power of her creator, stripped of all self-will!
I'll go after him! While I'm gone, pack up all of this. Especially that flash bomb.

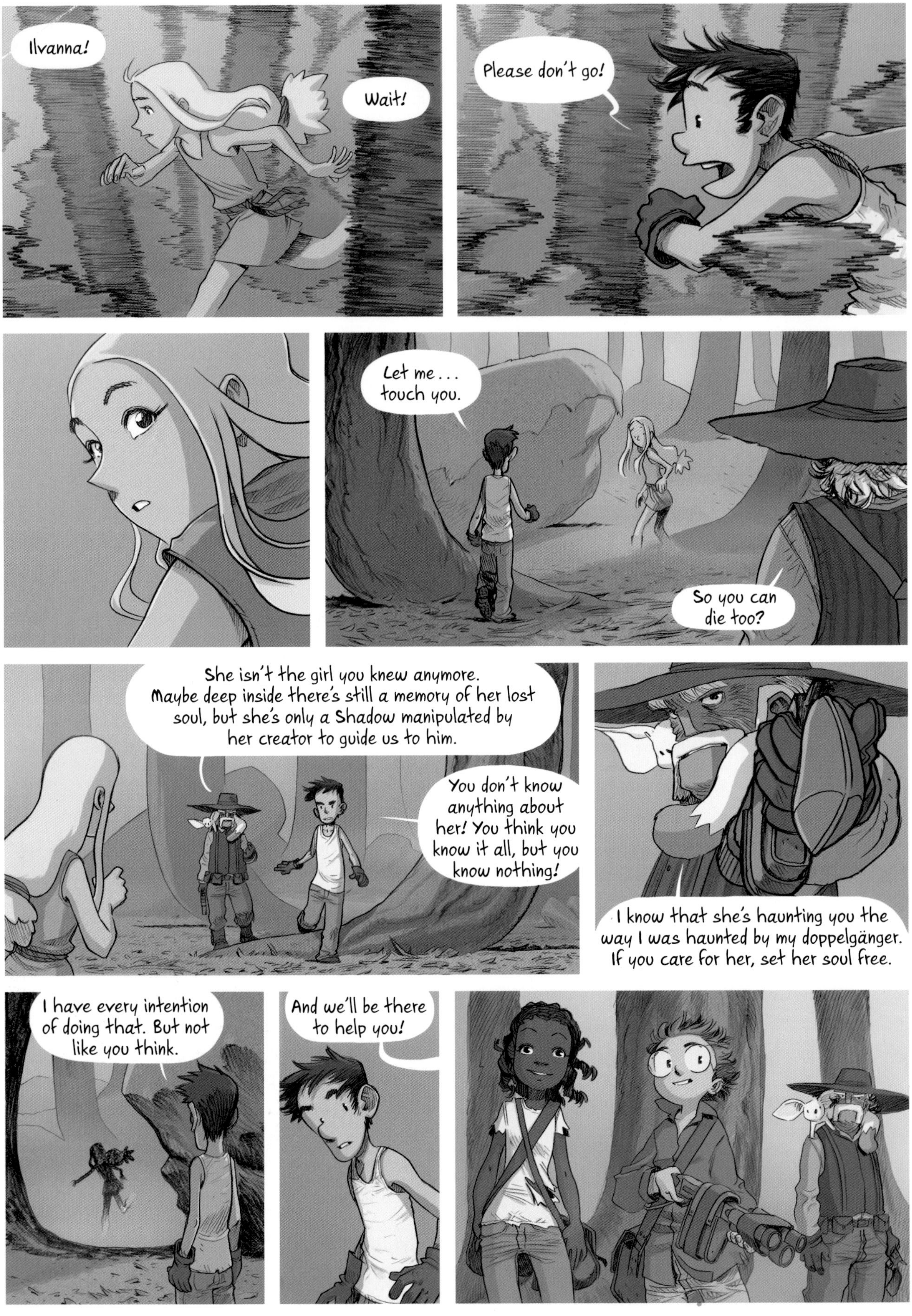
Ilvanna!
Wait!
Please don't go!
Let me . . . touch you.
So you can die too?
She isn't the girl you knew anymore. Maybe deep inside there's still a memory of her lost soul, but she's only a Shadow manipulated by her creator to guide us to him.
You don't know anything about her! You think you know it all, but you know nothing!
I know that she's haunting you the way I was haunted by my doppelgänger. If you care for her, set her soul free.
I have every intention of doing that. But not like you think.
And we'll be there to help you!

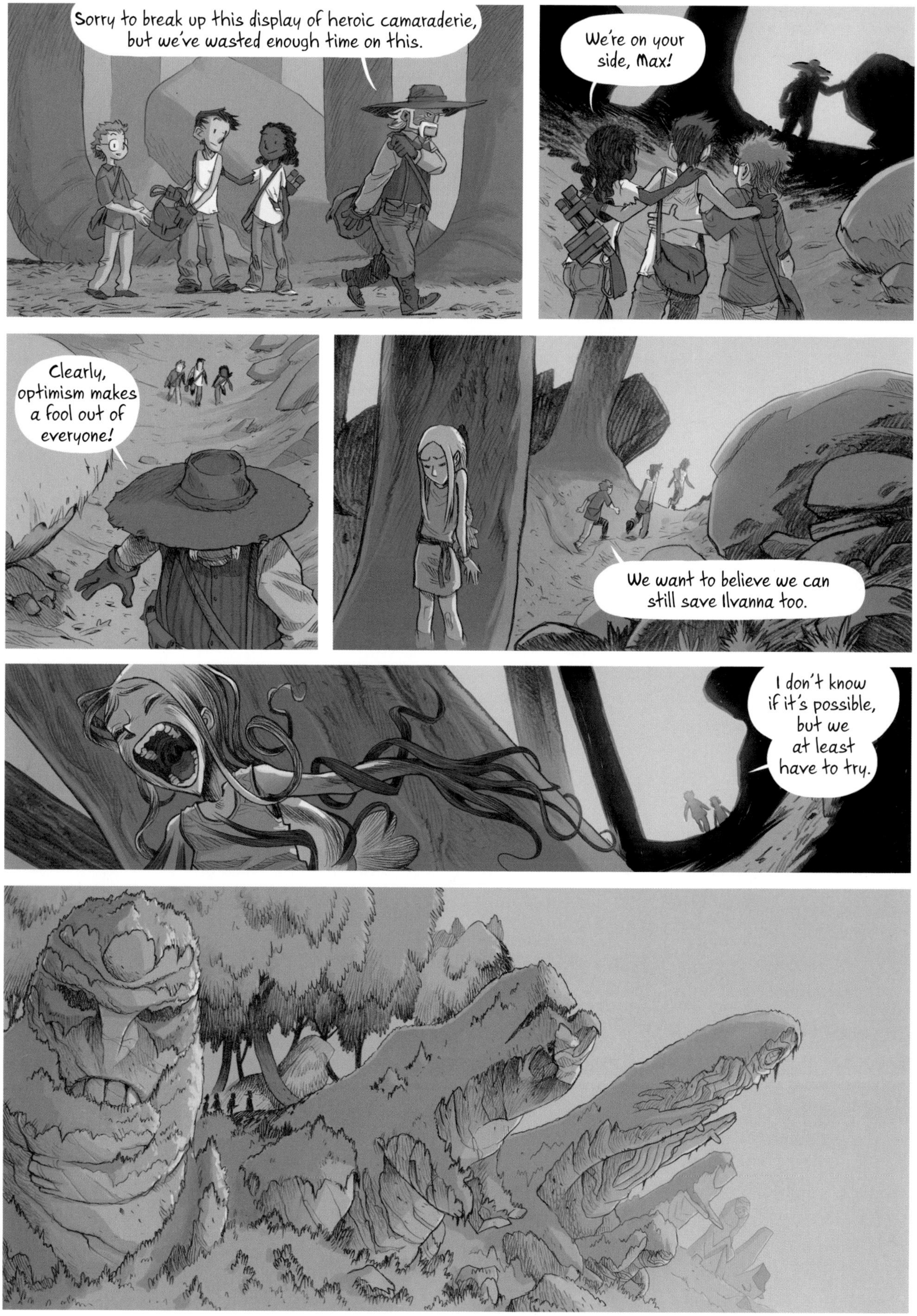

Sorry to break up this display of heroic camaraderie, but we've wasted enough time on this.
We're on your side, Max!
Clearly, optimism makes a fool out of everyone!
We want to believe we can still save Ilvanna too.
I don't know if it's possible, but we at least have to try.

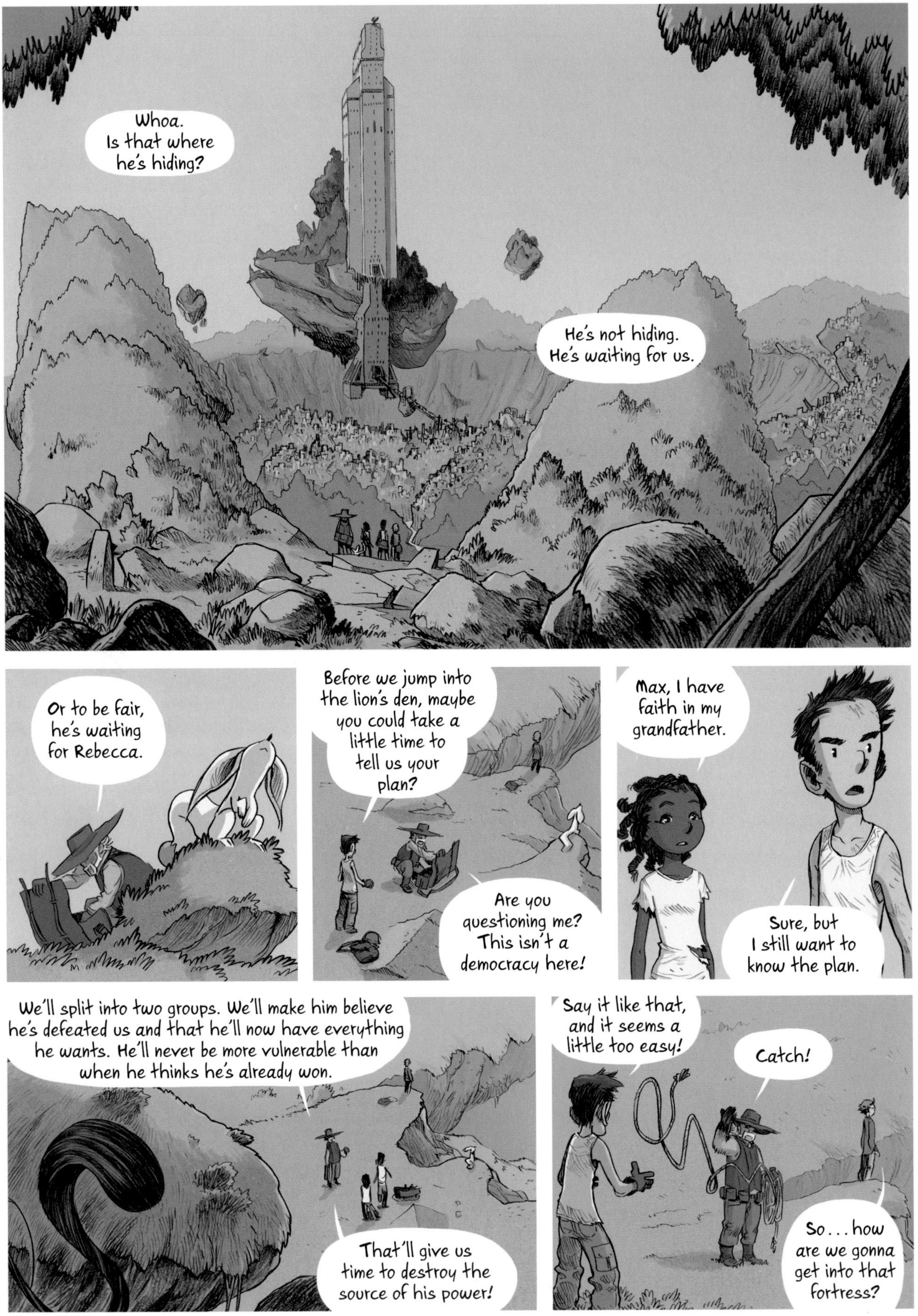
Whoa. Is that where he's hiding?
He's not hiding. He's waiting for us.
Or to be fair, he's waiting for Rebecca.
Before we jump into the lion's den, maybe you could take a little time to tell us your plan?
Are you questioning me? This isn't a democracy here!
Max, I have faith in my grandfather.
Sure, but I still want to know the plan.
We'll split into two groups. We'll make him believe he's defeated us and that he'll now have everything he wants. He'll never be more vulnerable than when he thinks he's already won.
That'll give us time to destroy the source of his power!
Say it like that, and it seems a little too easy!
Catch!
So... how are we gonna get into that fortress?

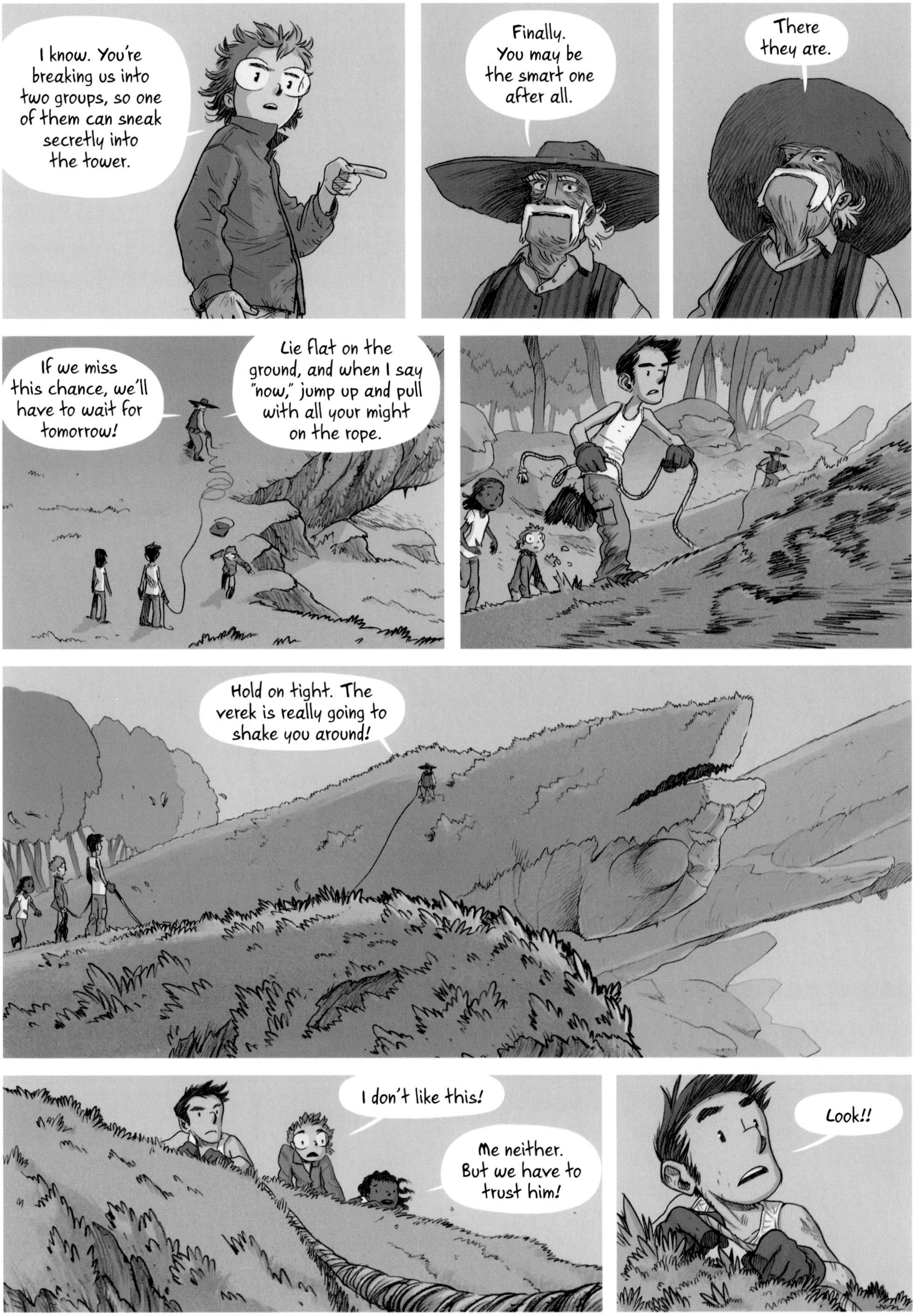
I know. You're breaking us into two groups, so one of them can sneak secretly into the tower.
Finally. You may be the smart one after all.
There they are.
If we miss this chance, we'll have to wait for tomorrow!
Lie flat on the ground, and when I say "now," jump up and pull with all your might on the rope.
Hold on tight. The verek is really going to shake you around!
I don't like this!
Me neither. But we have to trust him!
Look!!

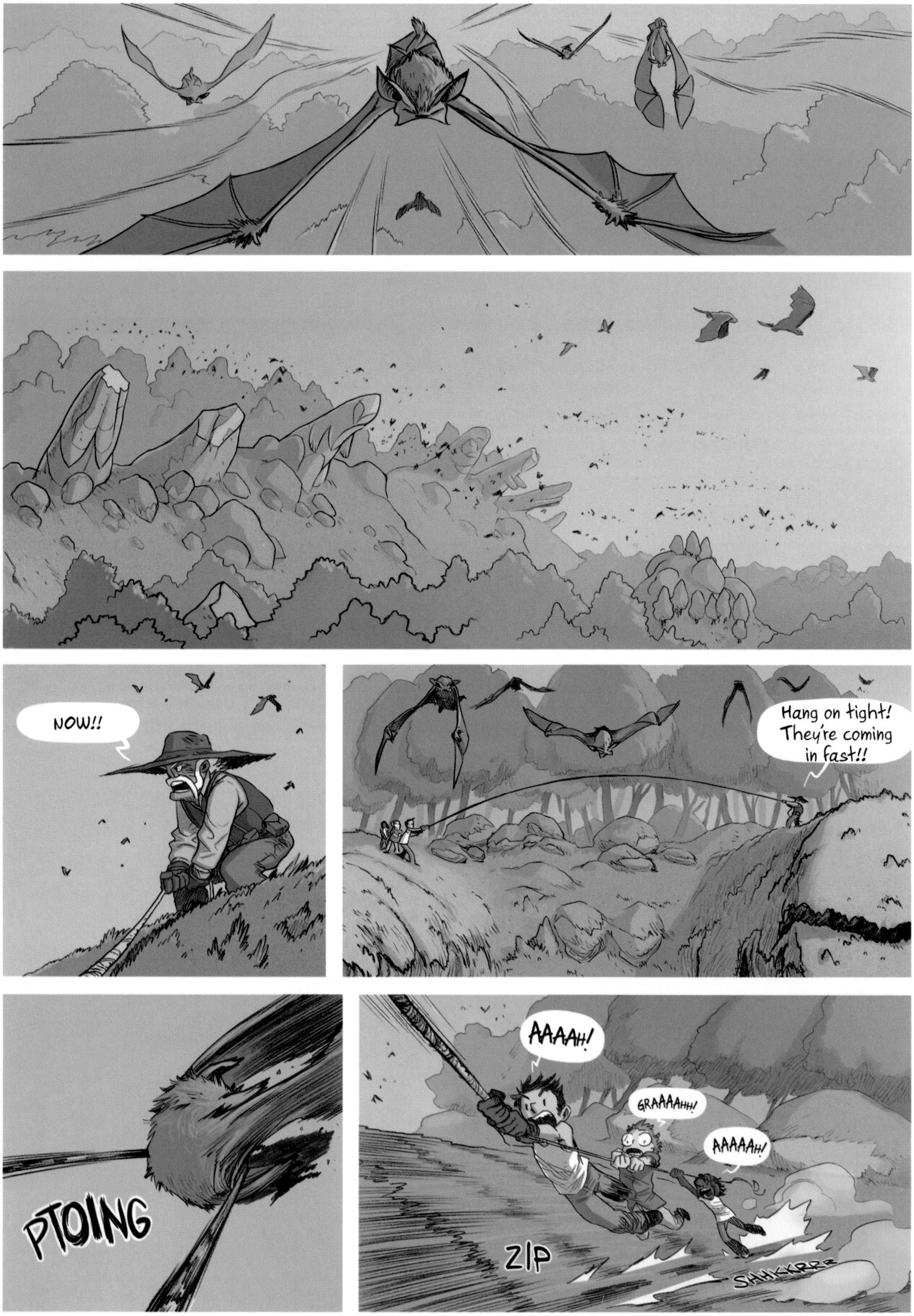
NOW!!
Hang on tight! They're coming in fast!!
PTOING
AAAAH!
GRAAAAHH!
AAAAAH!
ZIP
SHHKKRRR

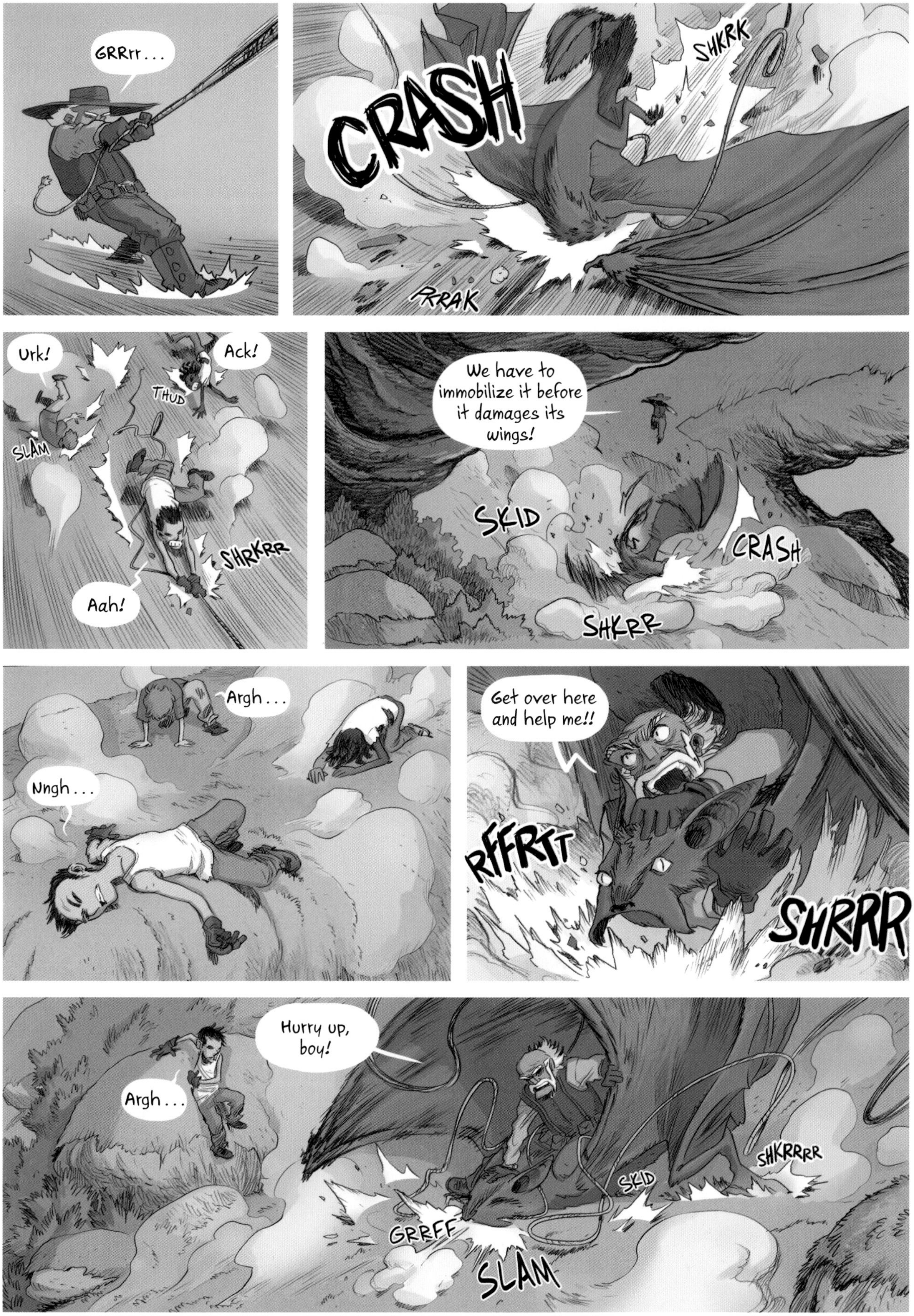

GRRrr...
CRASH
SHRKK
RRAK
Urk!
Ack!
THUD
SLAM
SHRKRR
Aah!
We have to immobilize it before it damages its wings!
SKID
CRASH
SHKRR
Argh...
Nngh...
Get over here and help me!!
RFFRTT
SHRRR
Hurry up, boy!
Argh...
SHKRRRR
SKID
GRRFF
SLAM

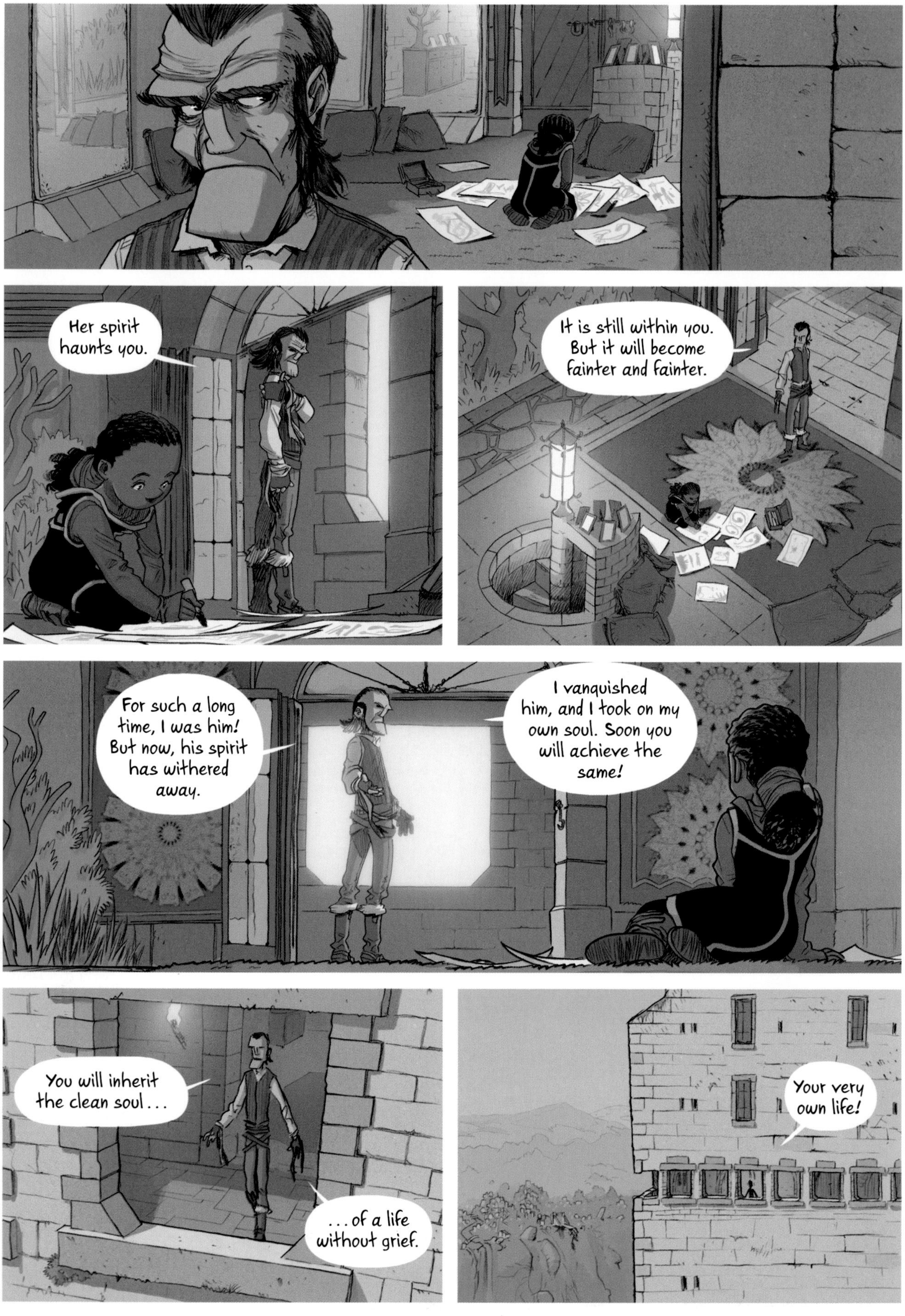
Her spirit haunts you.
It is still within you. But it will become fainter and fainter.
For such a long time, I was him! But now, his spirit has withered away.
I vanquished him, and I took on my own soul. Soon you will achieve the same!
You will inherit the clean soul . . .
. . . of a life without grief.
Your very own life!

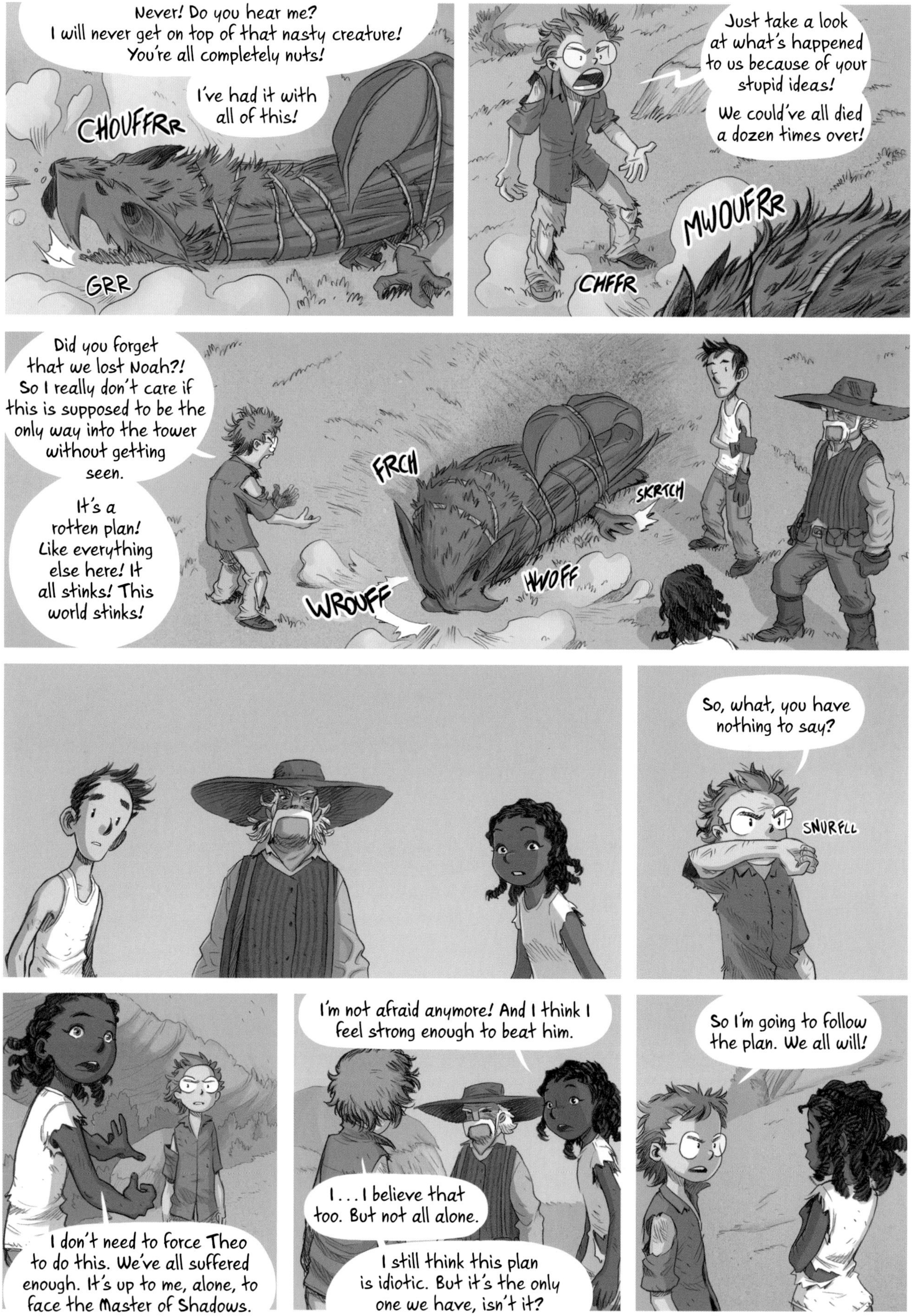
Never! Do you hear me? I will never get on top of that nasty creature! You're all completely nuts!
I've had it with all of this!
CHOUFFRR
GRR
Just take a look at what's happened to us because of your stupid ideas!
We could've all died a dozen times over!
MWOUFRR
CHFFR
Did you forget that we lost Noah?! So I really don't care if this is supposed to be the only way into the tower without getting seen.
It's a rotten plan! Like everything else here! It all stinks! This world stinks!
FRCH
SKRTCH
HWOFF
WROUFF
So, what, you have nothing to say?
SNURFLL
I don't need to force Theo to do this. We've all suffered enough. It's up to me, alone, to face the Master of Shadows.
I'm not afraid anymore! And I think I feel strong enough to beat him.
I . . . I believe that too. But not all alone.
I still think this plan is idiotic. But it's the only one we have, isn't it?
So I'm going to follow the plan. We all will!

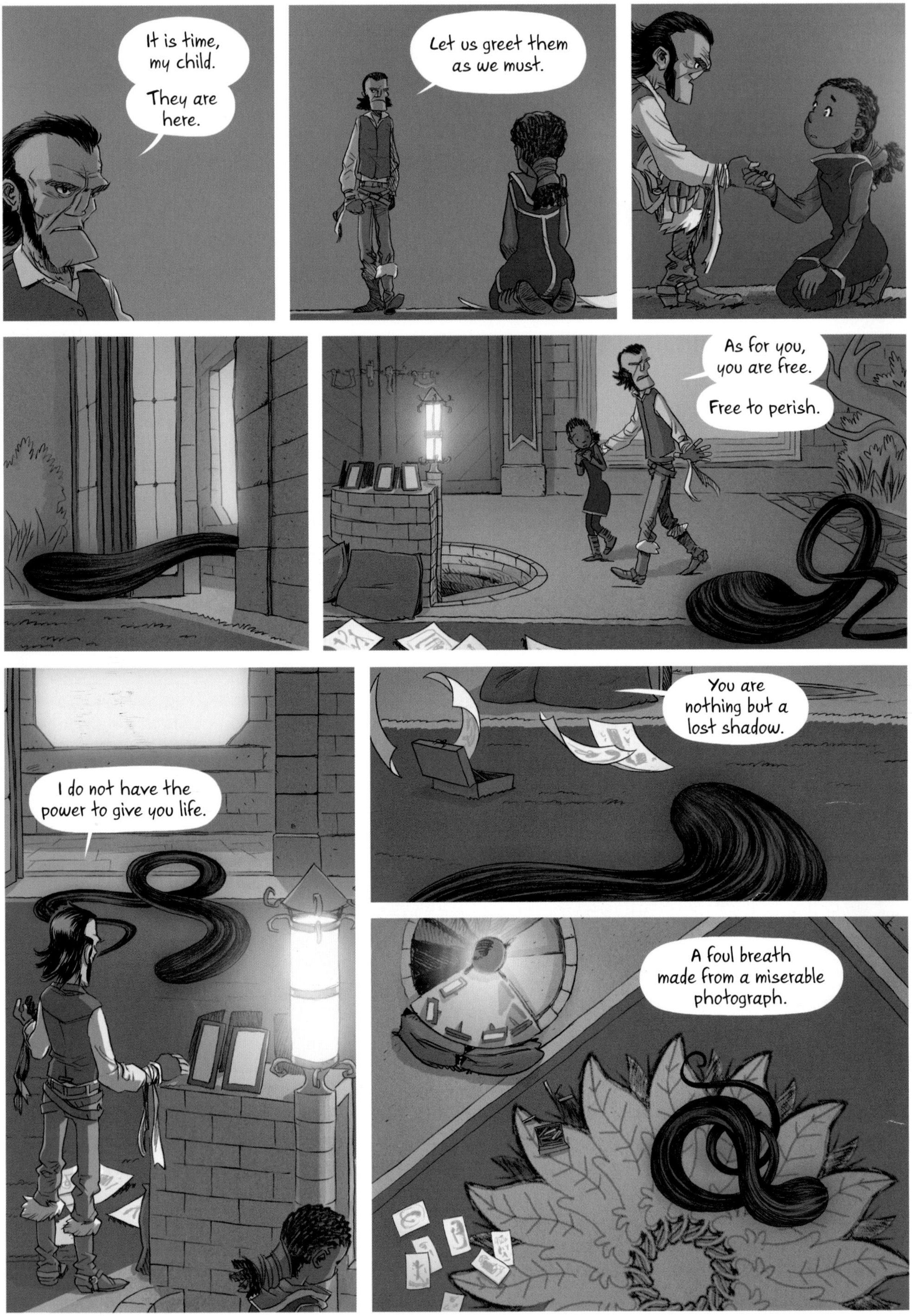

It is time, my child.
They are here.
Let us greet them as we must.
As for you, you are free.
Free to perish.
I do not have the power to give you life.
You are nothing but a lost shadow.
A foul breath made from a miserable photograph.

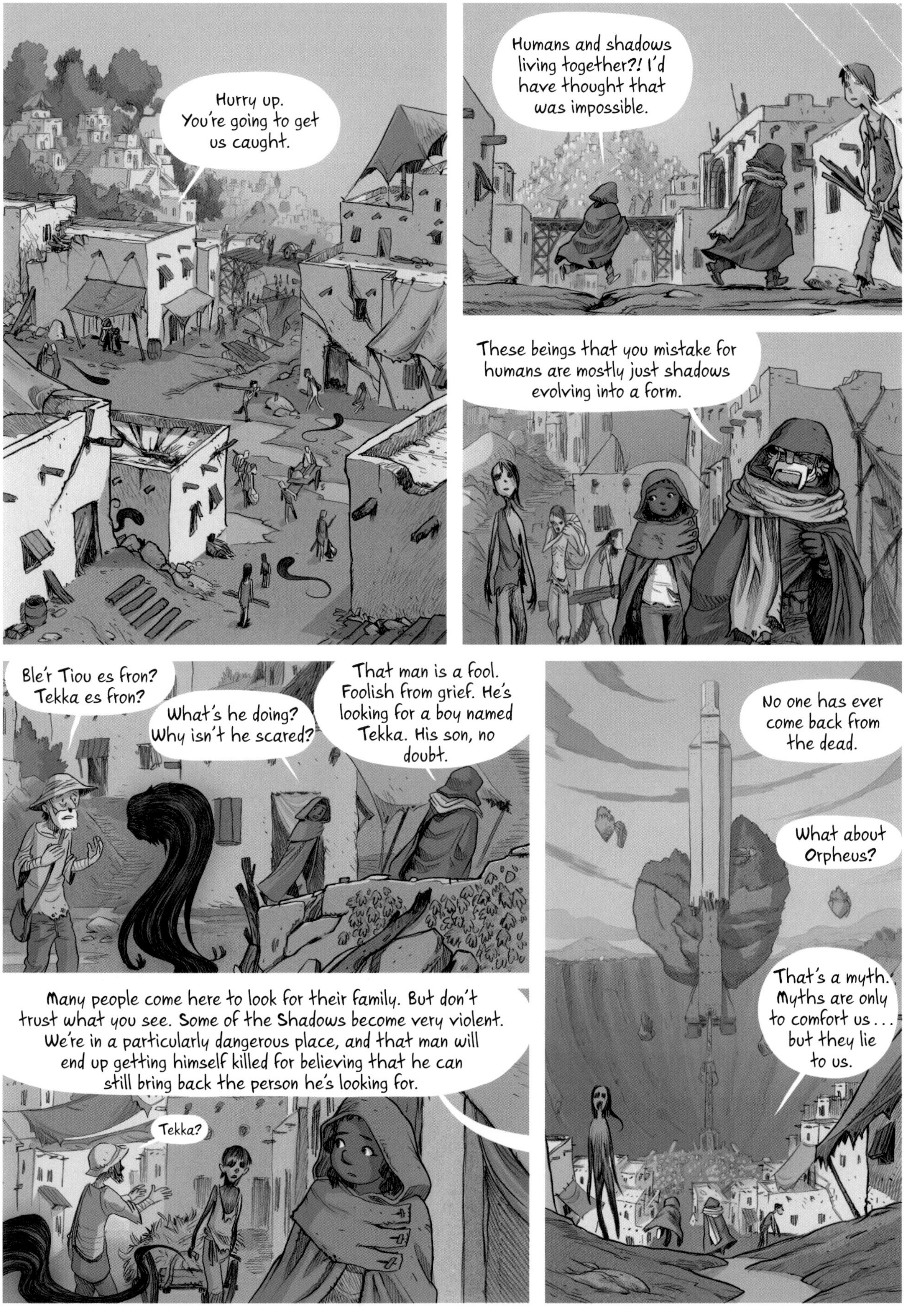
Hurry up. You're going to get us caught.
Humans and shadows living together?! I'd have thought that was impossible.
These beings that you mistake for humans are mostly just shadows evolving into a form.
Ble'r Tiou es fron? Tekka es fron?
What's he doing? Why isn't he scared?
That man is a fool. Foolish from grief. He's looking for a boy named Tekka. His son, no doubt.
Many people come here to look for their family. But don't trust what you see. Some of the Shadows become very violent. We're in a particularly dangerous place, and that man will end up getting himself killed for believing that he can still bring back the person he's looking for.
Tekka?
No one has ever come back from the dead.
What about Orpheus?
That's a myth. Myths are only to comfort us . . . but they lie to us.

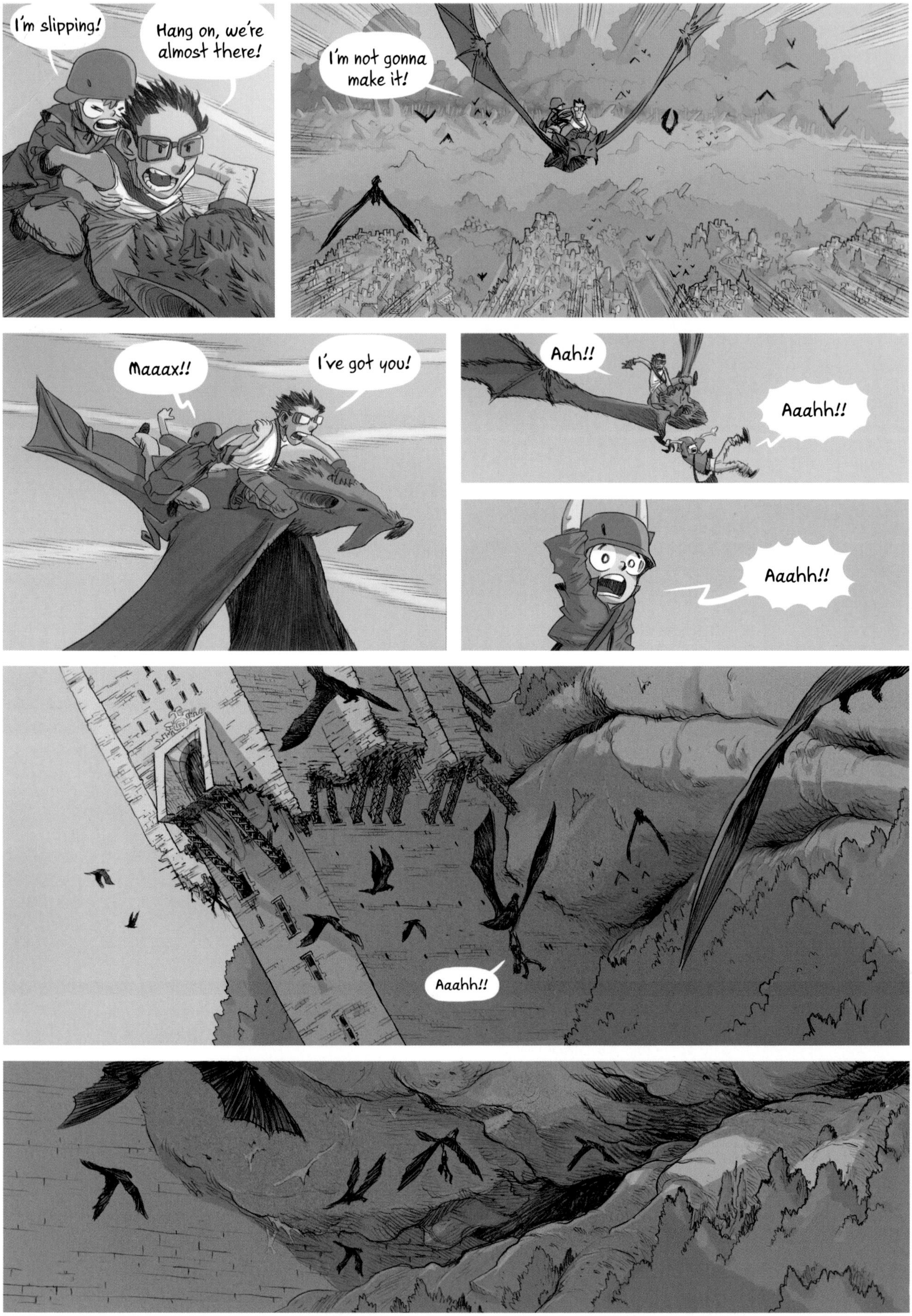
I'm slipping!
Hang on, we're almost there!
I'm not gonna make it!
Maaax!!
I've got you!
Aah!!
Aaahh!!
Aaahh!!
Aaahh!!

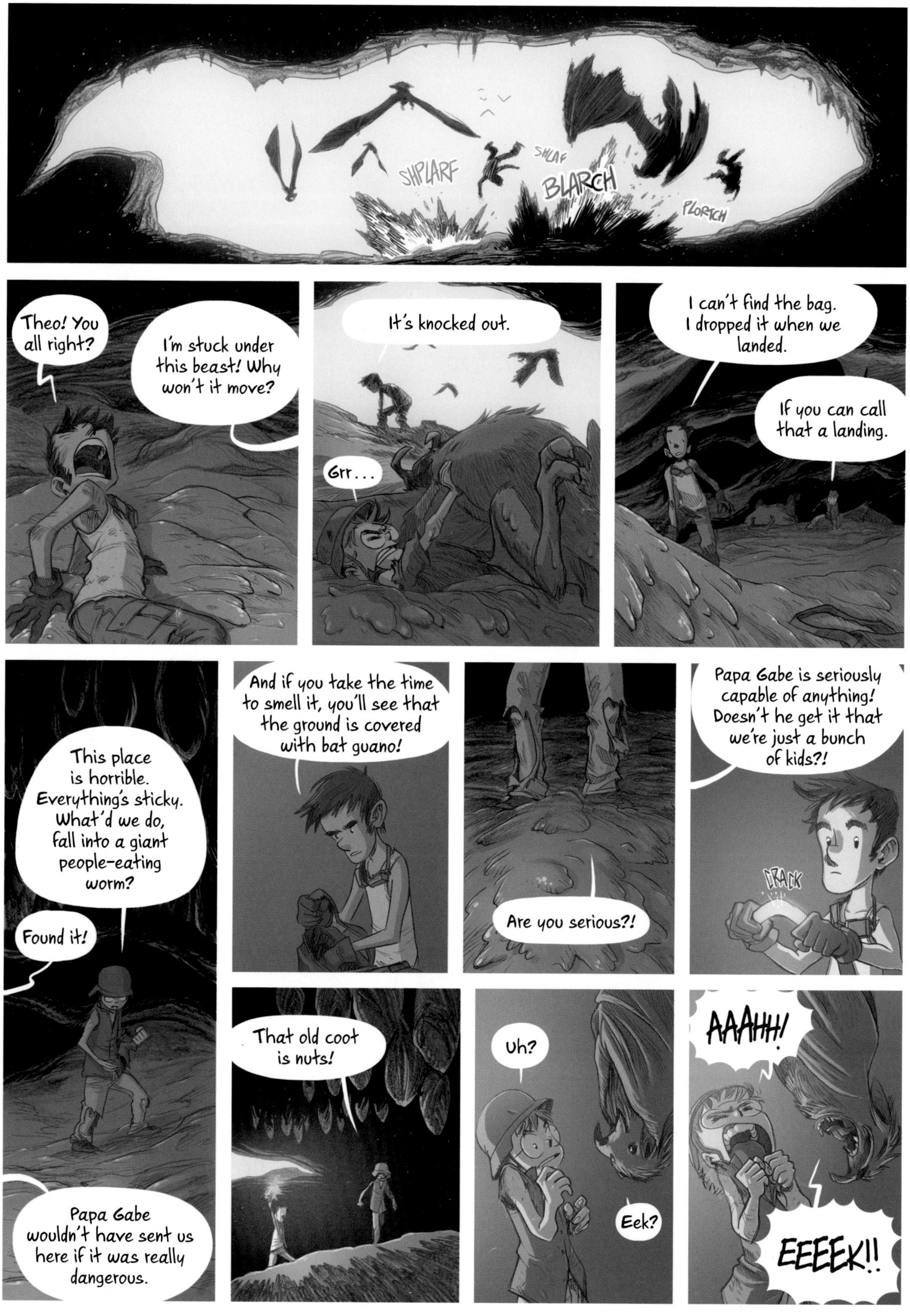
SHPLARF
SHLAF
BLARCH
PLORTCH
Theo! You all right?
I'm stuck under this beast! Why won't it move?
It's knocked out.
Grr...
I can't find the bag. I dropped it when we landed.
If you can call that a landing.
This place is horrible. Everything's sticky. What'd we do, fall into a giant people-eating worm?
Found it!
Papa Gabe wouldn't have sent us here if it was really dangerous.
And if you take the time to smell it, you'll see that the ground is covered with bat guano!
Are you serious?!
Papa Gabe is seriously capable of anything! Doesn't he get it that we're just a bunch of kids?!
CRACK
That old coot is nuts!
Uh?
Eek?
AAAHH!
EEEEK!!

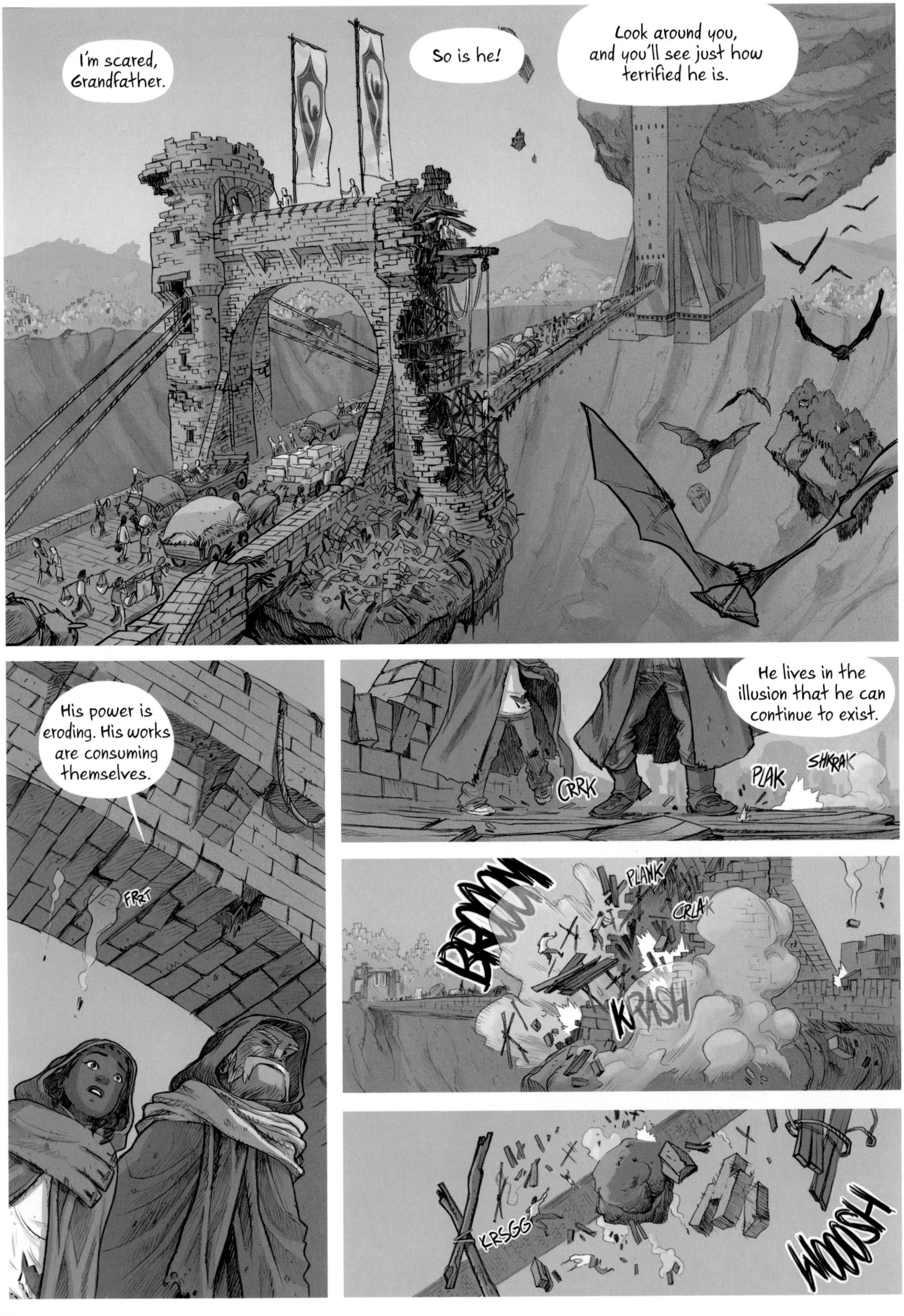
I'm scared, Grandfather.
So is he!
Look around you, and you'll see just how terrified he is.
His power is eroding. His works are consuming themselves.
FRZT
He lives in the illusion that he can continue to exist.
CRRK
PLAK
SHKRAK
BROOOM
PLANK
CRLAK
KRASH
KRSGG
WOOSH

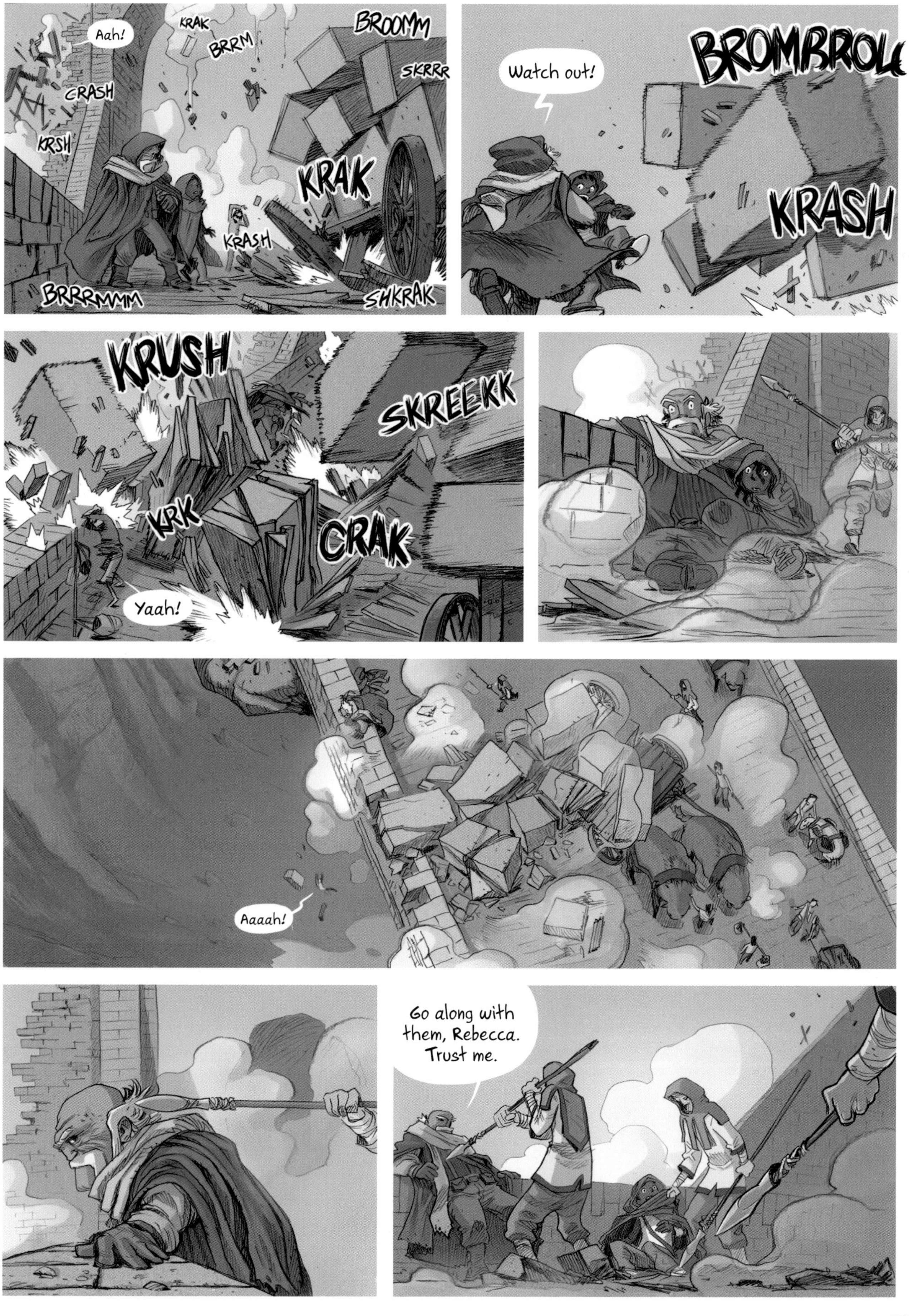
Aah!
KRAK
BRRM
CRASH
KRSH
BROOMM
SKRRR
KRAK
KRASH
BRRRMMM
SHKRAK
Watch out!
BROMBROU
KRASH
KRUSH
SKREEKK
KRK
CRAK
Yaah!
Aaaah!
Go along with them, Rebecca. Trust me.

We need to hurry up and find the way out, that's for sure!

Calm down. They're more scared of us than we are of them.

Yeah, I don't think so. That one just pooped on me.

Then quit bothering them!

A breeze—I just felt a current of air!

Uggh! He's licking me!

SHLUURPCHH

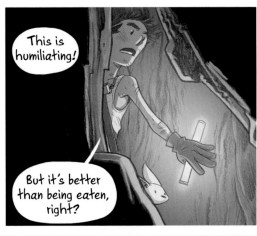

This is humiliating!

But it's better than being eaten, right?

This must be the tower's subbasement.

We can get through here. It looks safe!

Let's get out of here as fast as possible.

There!

You're kidding, right?!

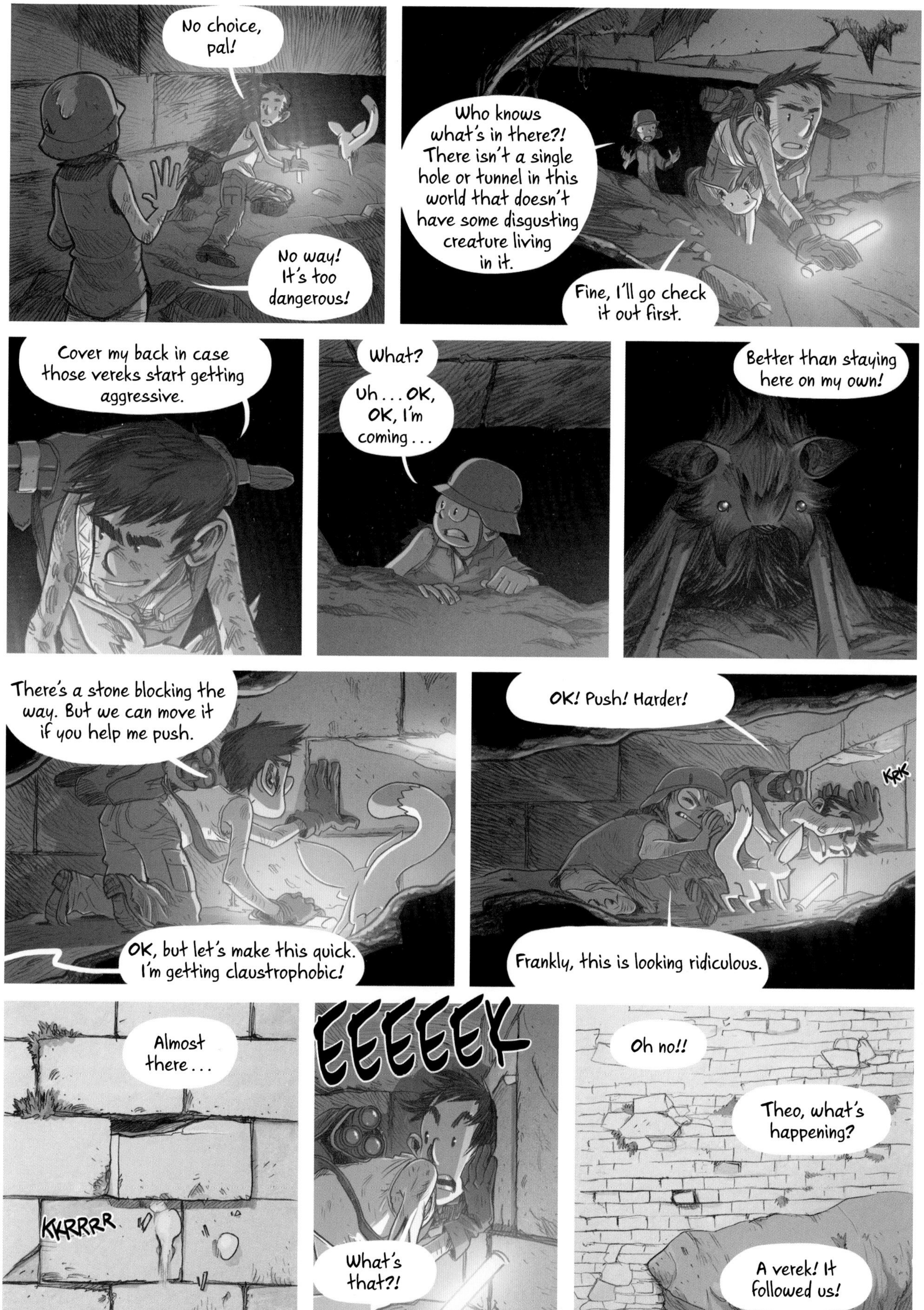

No choice, pal!
No way! It's too dangerous!
Who knows what's in there?! There isn't a single hole or tunnel in this world that doesn't have some disgusting creature living in it.
Fine, I'll go check it out first.
Cover my back in case those vereks start getting aggressive.
What?
Uh . . . OK, OK, I'm coming . . .
Better than staying here on my own!
There's a stone blocking the way. But we can move it if you help me push.
OK, but let's make this quick. I'm getting claustrophobic!
OK! Push! Harder!
KRK
Frankly, this is looking ridiculous.
Almost there . . .
KKRRRR
EEEEEEK
What's that?!
Oh no!!
Theo, what's happening?
A verek! It followed us!

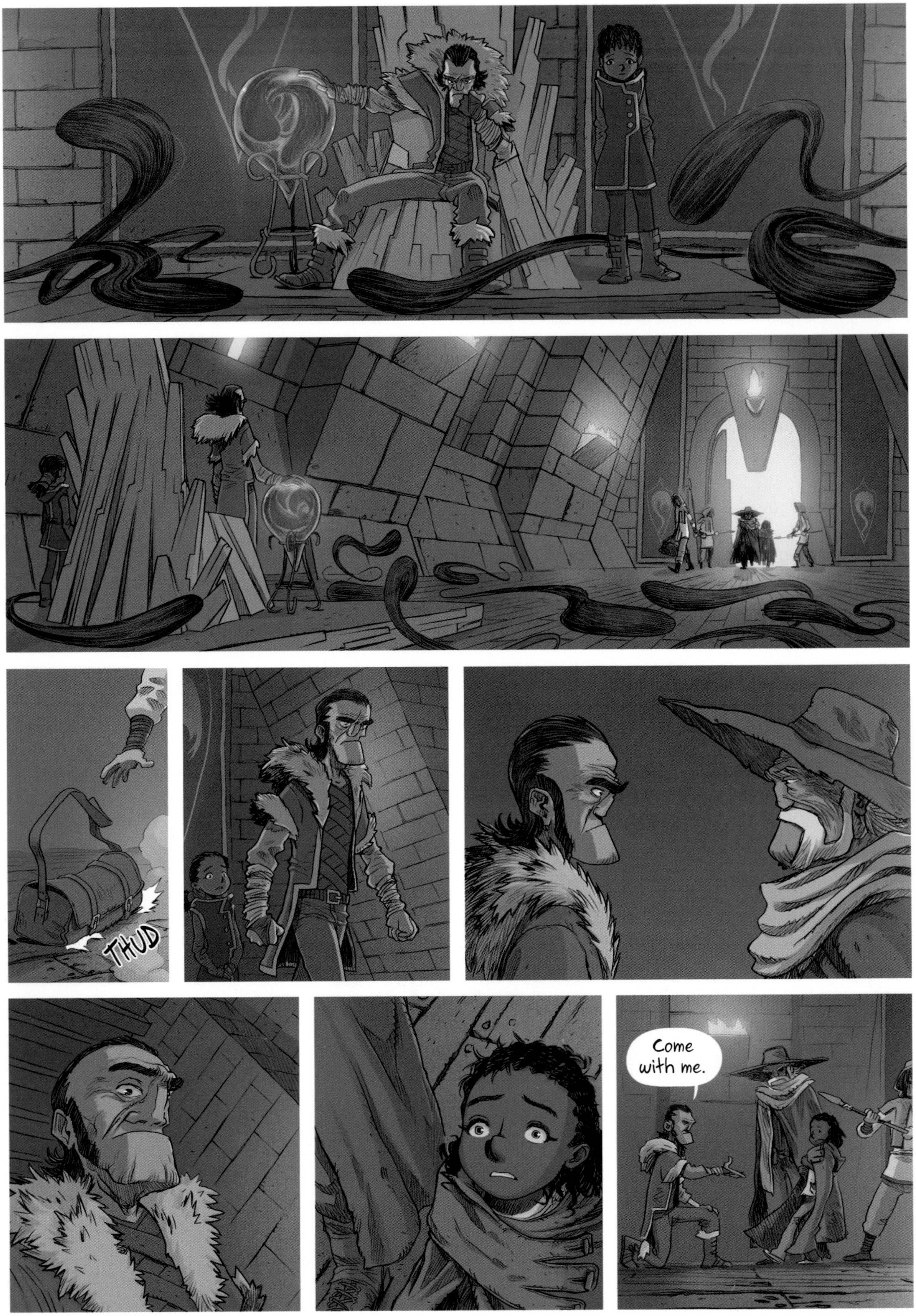
THUD
Come with me.

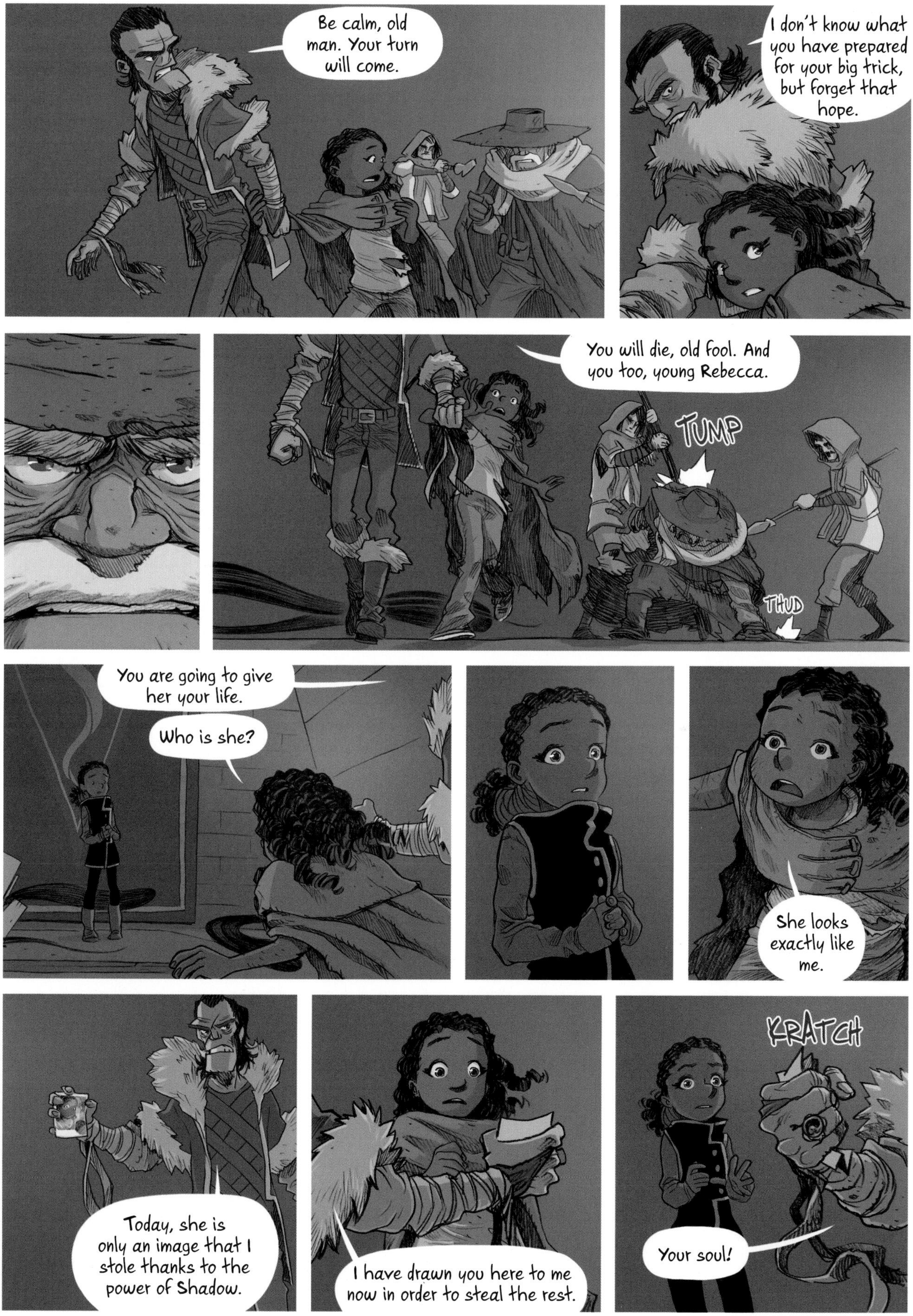
Be calm, old man. Your turn will come.
I don't know what you have prepared for your big trick, but forget that hope.
You will die, old fool. And you too, young Rebecca.
TUMP
THUD
You are going to give her your life.
Who is she?
She looks exactly like me.
Today, she is only an image that I stole thanks to the power of Shadow.
I have drawn you here to me now in order to steal the rest.
KRATCH
Your soul!

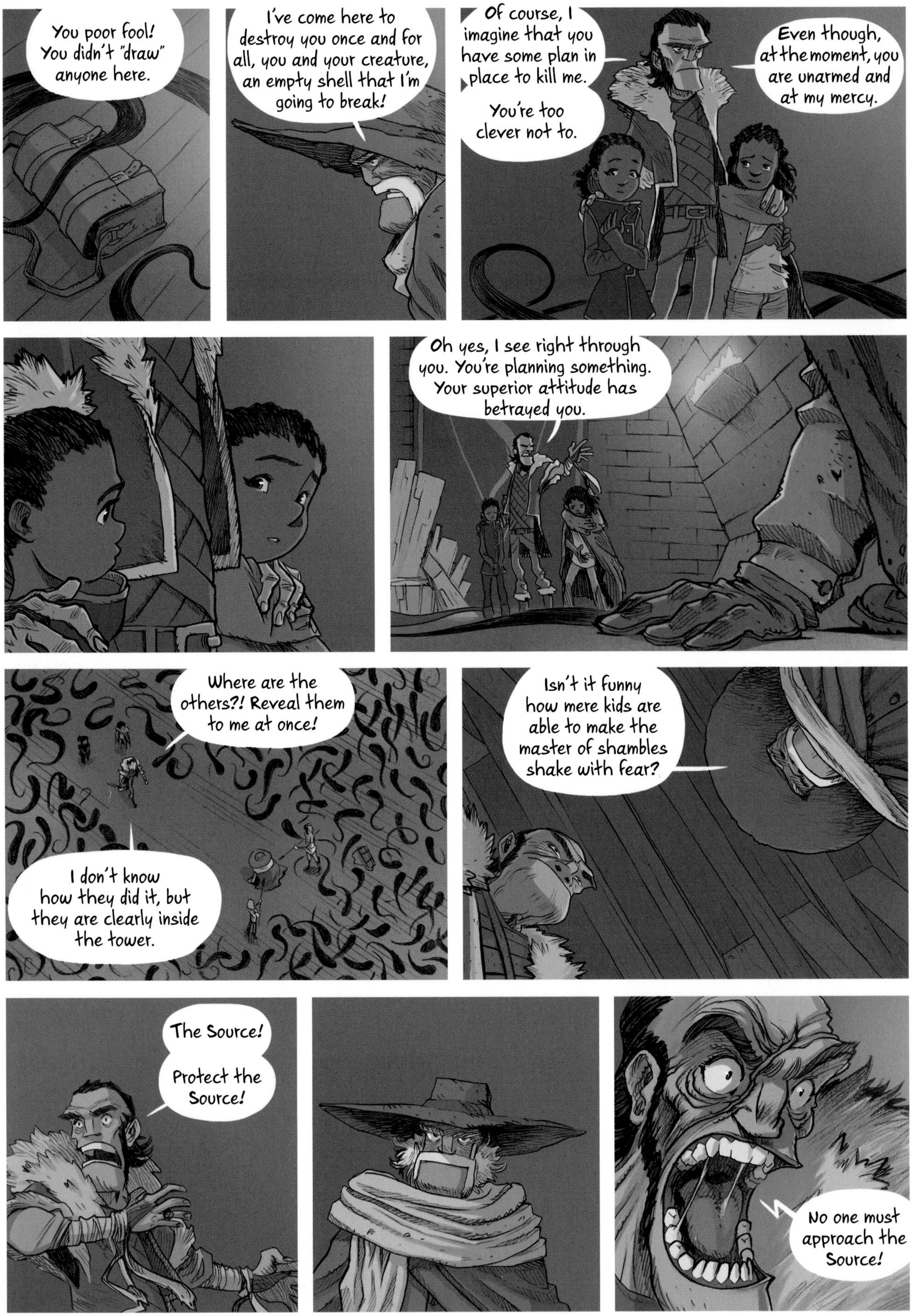

You poor fool! You didn't "draw" anyone here.
I've come here to destroy you once and for all, you and your creature, an empty shell that I'm going to break!
Of course, I imagine that you have some plan in place to kill me.
You're too clever not to.
Even though, at the moment, you are unarmed and at my mercy.
Oh yes, I see right through you. You're planning something. Your superior attitude has betrayed you.
Where are the others?! Reveal them to me at once!
I don't know how they did it, but they are clearly inside the tower.
Isn't it funny how mere kids are able to make the master of shambles shake with fear?
The Source!
Protect the Source!
No one must approach the Source!

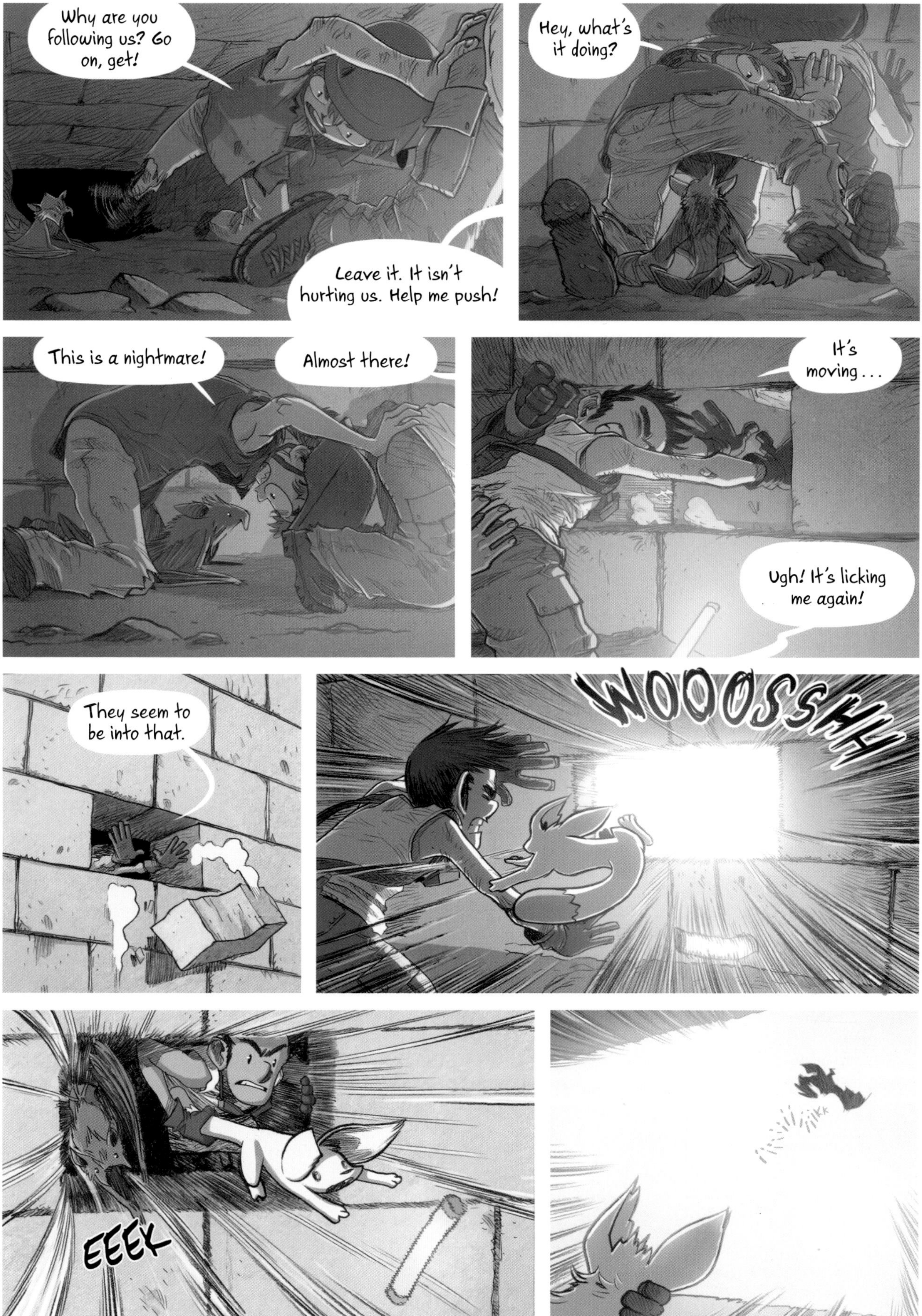
Why are you following us? Go on, get!
Hey, what's it doing?
Leave it. It isn't hurting us. Help me push!
This is a nightmare!
Almost there!
It's moving . . .
Ugh! It's licking me again!
They seem to be into that.
WOOOSSHH
EEEK

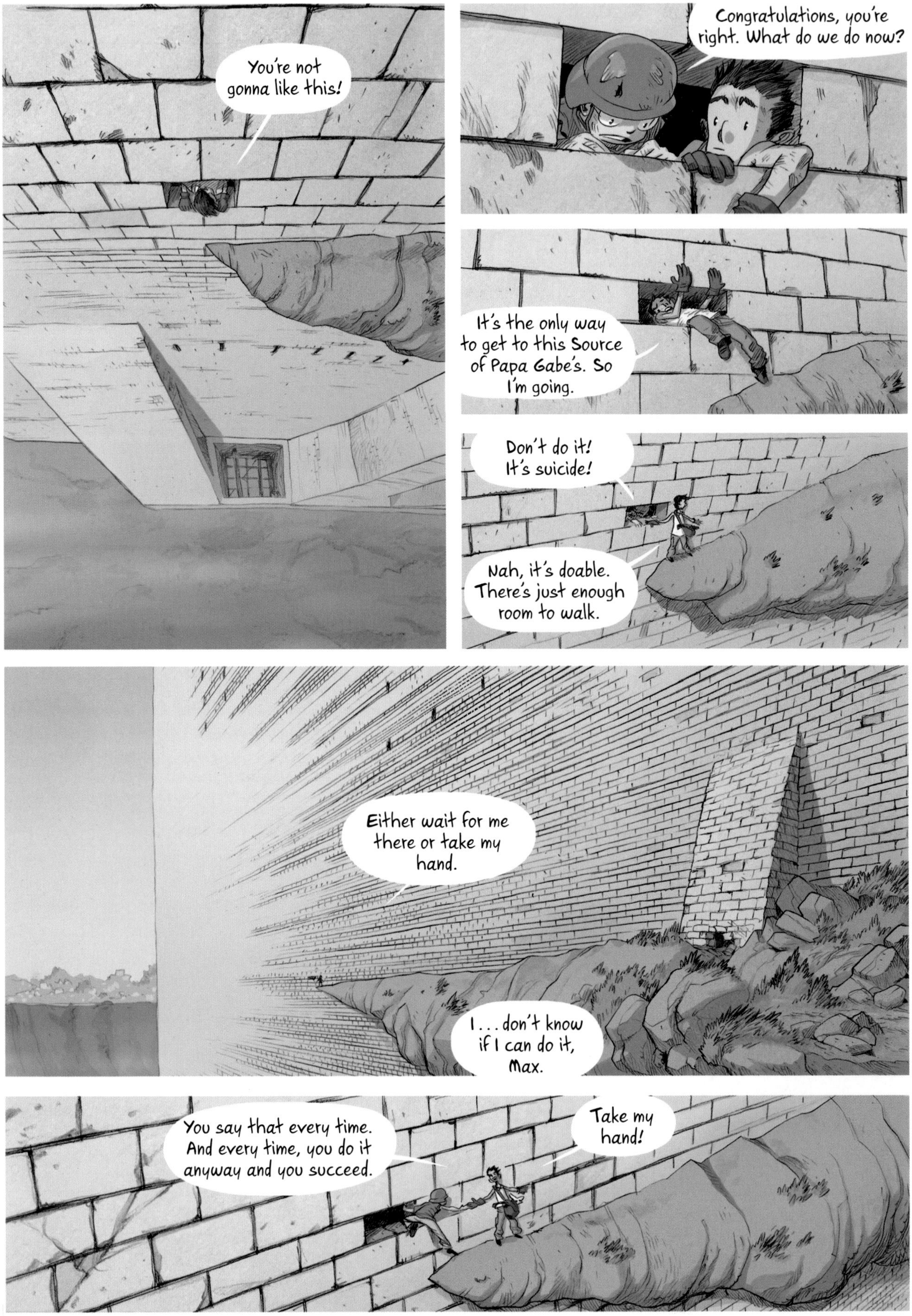

You're not gonna like this!
Congratulations, you're right. What do we do now?
It's the only way to get to this Source of Papa Gabe's. So I'm going.
Don't do it! It's suicide!
Nah, it's doable. There's just enough room to walk.
Either wait for me there or take my hand.
I... don't know if I can do it, Max.
You say that every time. And every time, you do it anyway and you succeed.
Take my hand!

I'm scared, Max! I can't feel my legs!

Me neither. I'm scared witless.

I'm scared more than I've ever been...

Not really what I was hoping to hear. I...I can't move.

...except maybe that time when my brother swore he was gonna break my arm...

...in revenge for one of his dumb pranks, I squirted a jar of mustard in his ear.

When he caught me, I was so scared I messed my pants. He was twisting my arm like you'd wring out a mop.

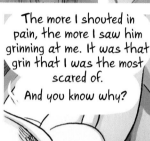

The more I shouted in pain, the more I saw him grinning at me. It was that grin that I was the most scared of.

And you know why?

Because right then I got it, that he was really trying to break my arm. It wasn't just a threat. He really wanted to do it.

And he only failed because he didn't know how to do it.

You did it, Theo! You did it!

Thanks...

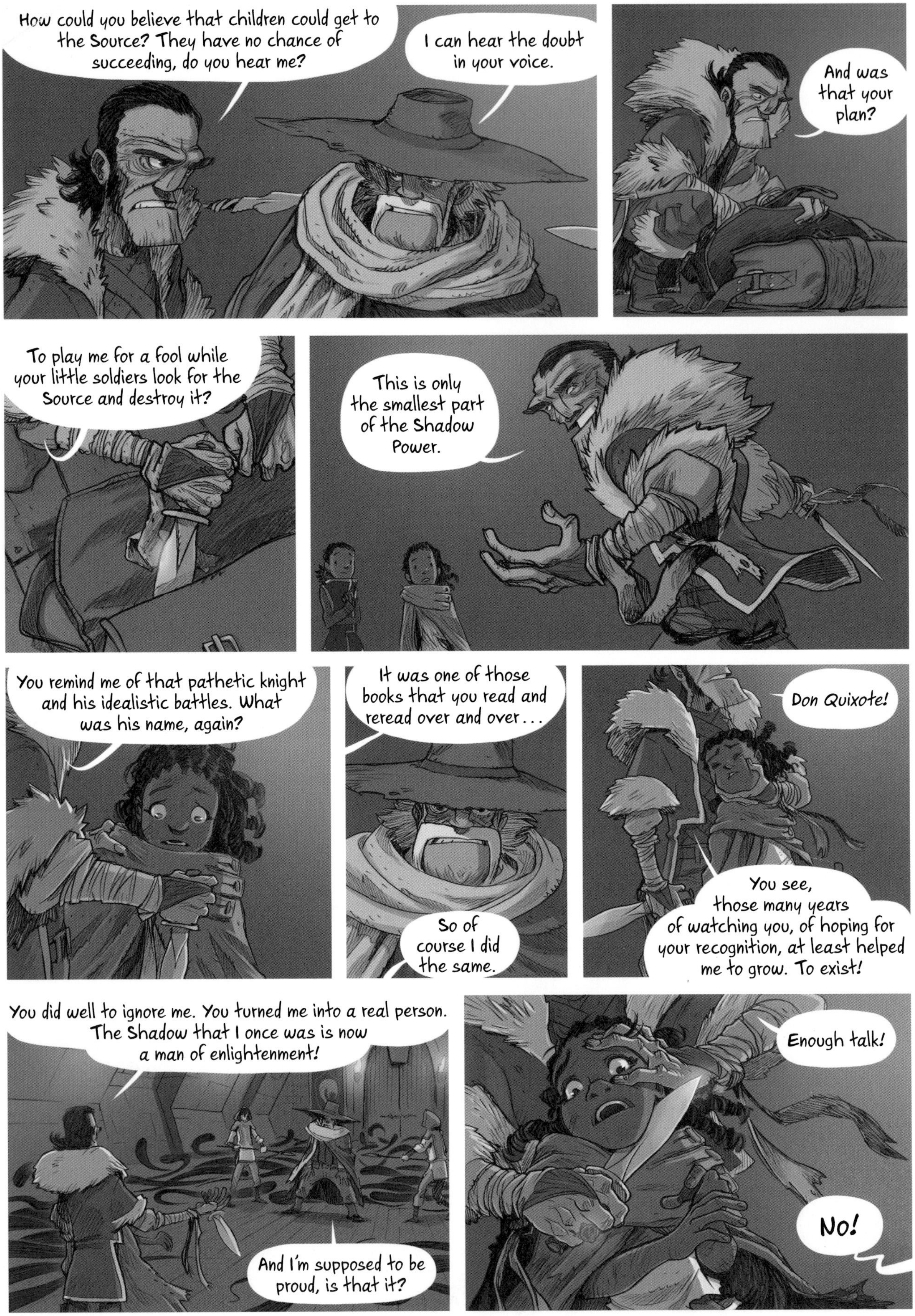
How could you believe that children could get to the Source? They have no chance of succeeding, do you hear me?
I can hear the doubt in your voice.
And was that your plan?
To play me for a fool while your little soldiers look for the Source and destroy it?
This is only the smallest part of the Shadow Power.
You remind me of that pathetic knight and his idealistic battles. What was his name, again?
It was one of those books that you read and reread over and over . . .
So of course I did the same.
Don Quixote!
You see, those many years of watching you, of hoping for your recognition, at least helped me to grow. To exist!
You did well to ignore me. You turned me into a real person. The Shadow that I once was is now a man of enlightenment!
And I'm supposed to be proud, is that it?
Enough talk!
No!

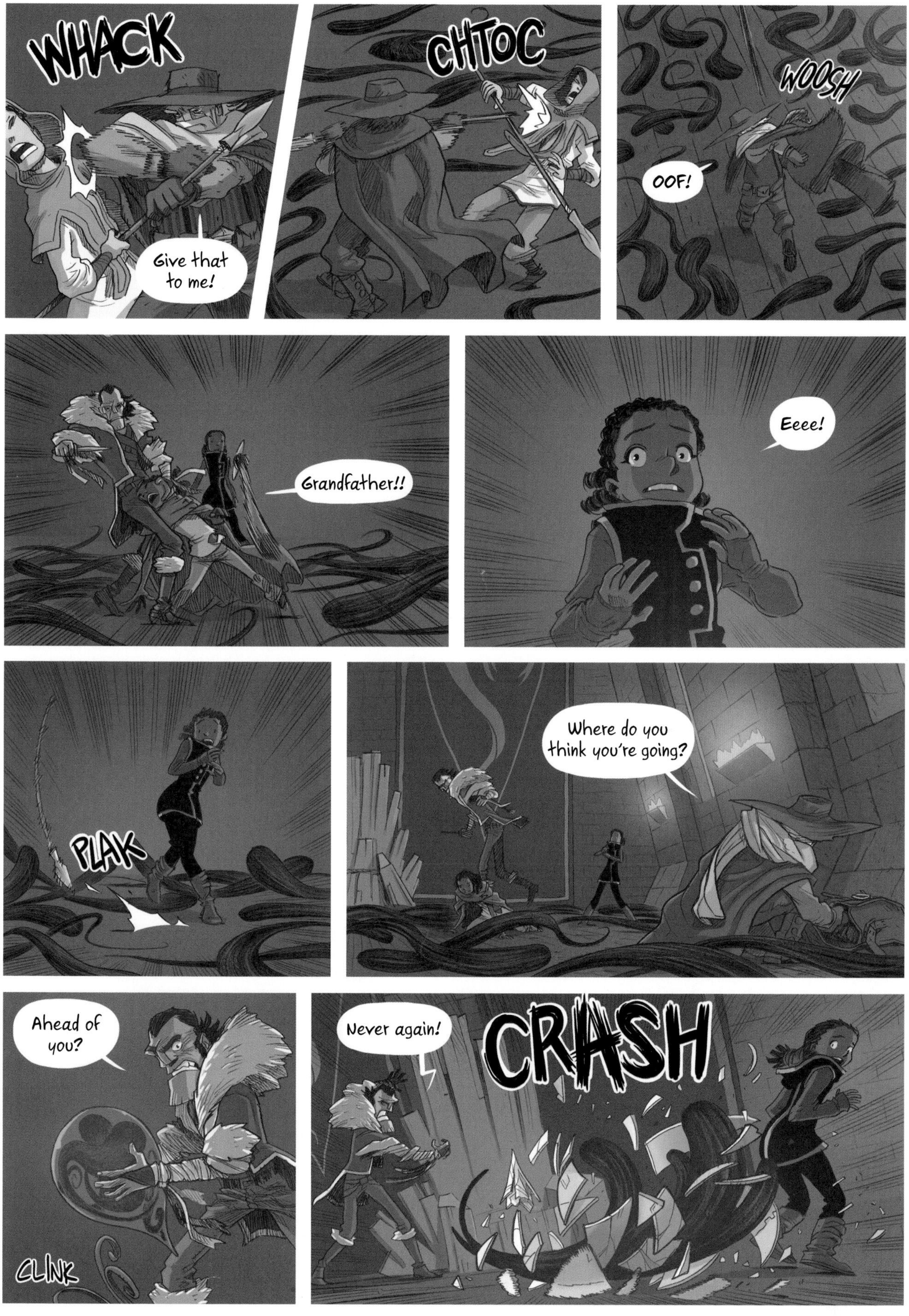
WHACK
Give that to me!
CHTOC
WOOSH
OOF!
Grandfather!!
Eeee!
PLAK
Where do you think you're going?
Ahead of you?
CLINK
Never again!
CRASH

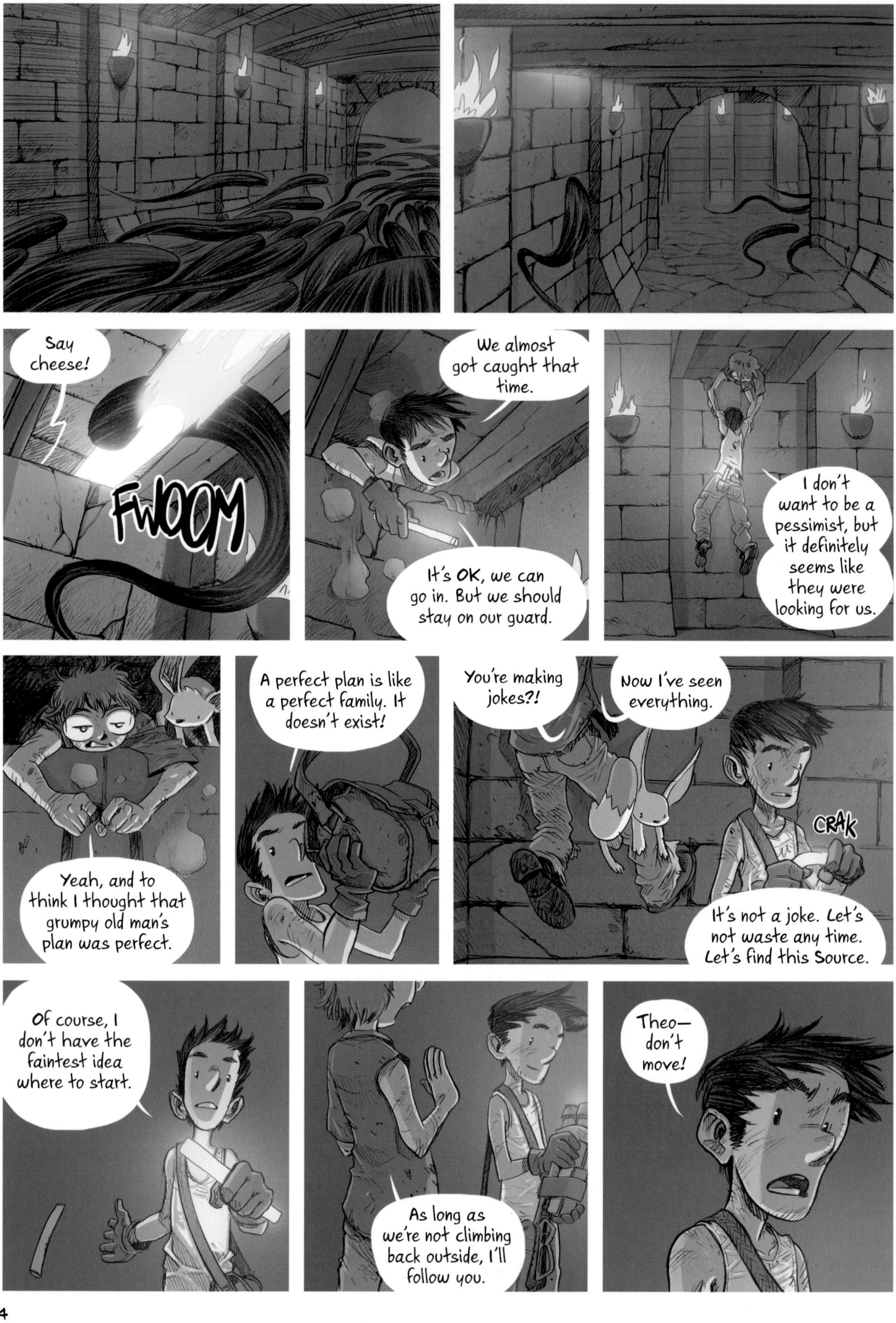
Say cheese!
FWOOM
We almost got caught that time.
It's OK, we can go in. But we should stay on our guard.
I don't want to be a pessimist, but it definitely seems like they were looking for us.
Yeah, and to think I thought that grumpy old man's plan was perfect.
A perfect plan is like a perfect family. It doesn't exist!
You're making jokes?!
Now I've seen everything.
CRAK
It's not a joke. Let's not waste any time. Let's find this Source.
Of course, I don't have the faintest idea where to start.
As long as we're not climbing back outside, I'll follow you.
Theo—don't move!

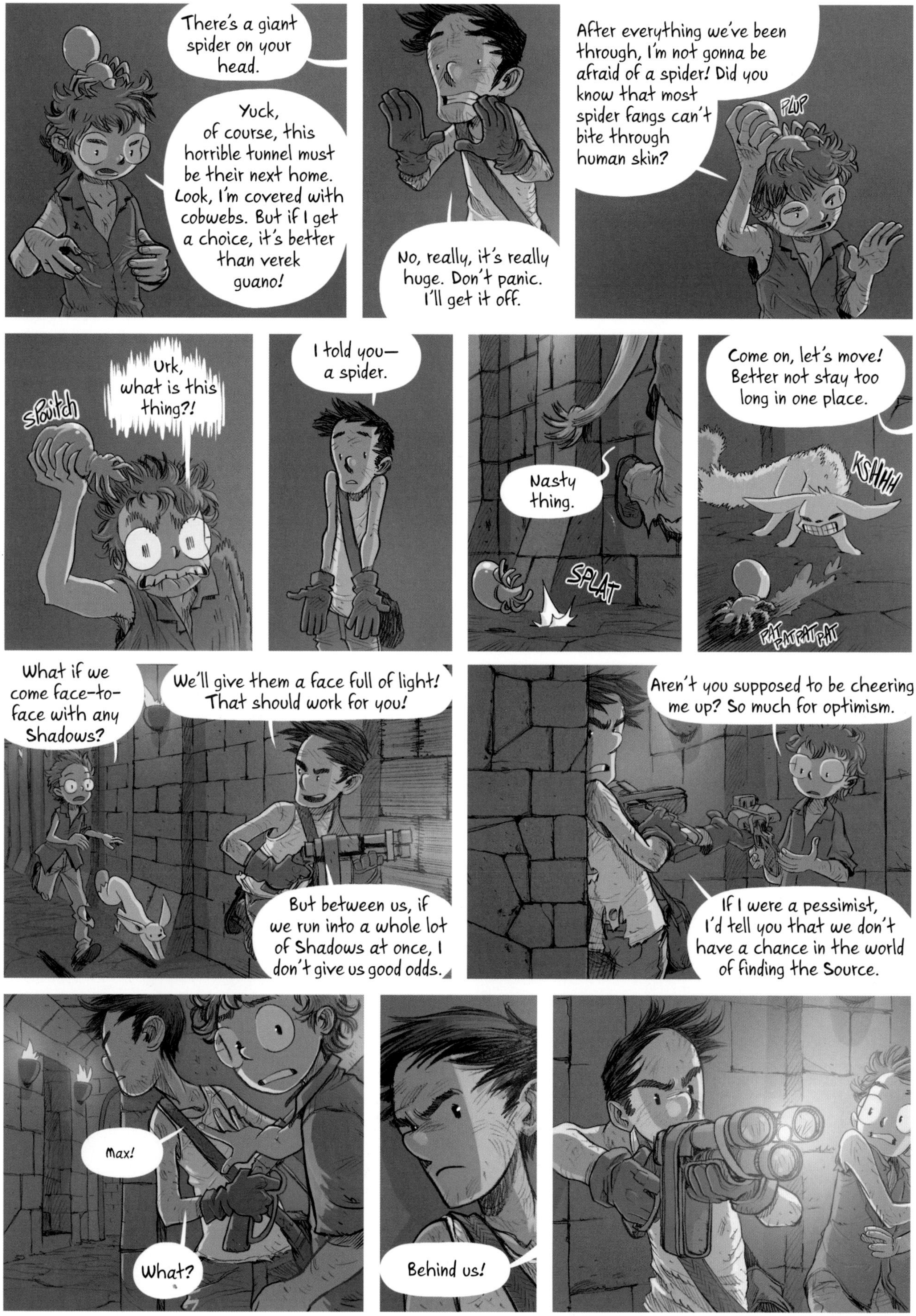

There's a giant spider on your head.
Yuck, of course, this horrible tunnel must be their next home. Look, I'm covered with cobwebs. But if I get a choice, it's better than verek guano!
No, really, it's really huge. Don't panic. I'll get it off.
After everything we've been through, I'm not gonna be afraid of a spider! Did you know that most spider fangs can't bite through human skin?
PLUP
SPOUITCH
Urk, what is this thing?!
I told you— a spider.
Nasty thing.
SPLAT
Come on, let's move! Better not stay too long in one place.
KSHHH
PAT PATPAT PAT
What if we come face-to-face with any Shadows?
We'll give them a face full of light! That should work for you!
But between us, if we run into a whole lot of Shadows at once, I don't give us good odds.
Aren't you supposed to be cheering me up? So much for optimism.
If I were a pessimist, I'd tell you that we don't have a chance in the world of finding the Source.
Max!
What?
Behind us!

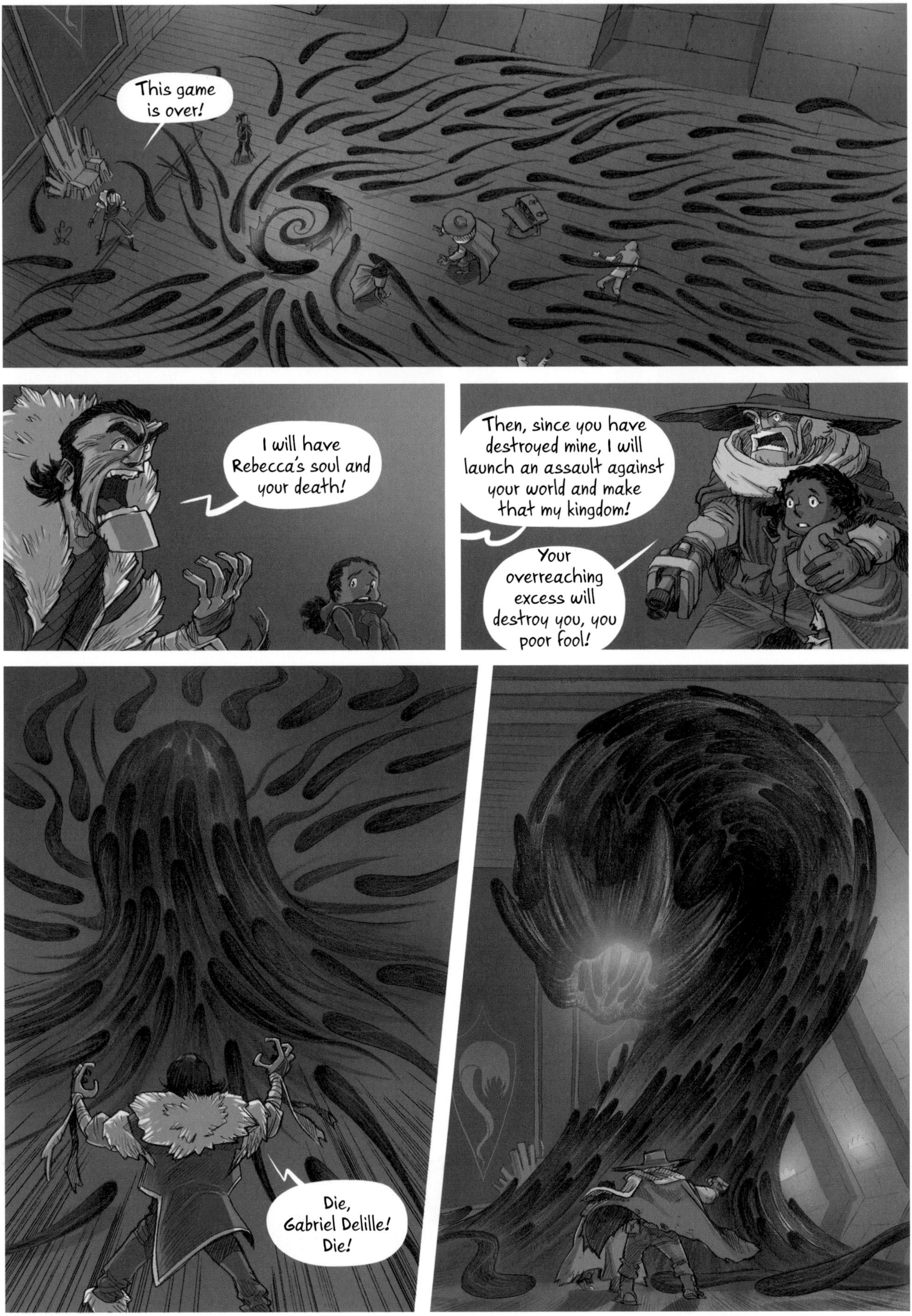
This game is over!
I will have Rebecca's soul and your death!
Then, since you have destroyed mine, I will launch an assault against your world and make that my kingdom!
Your overreaching excess will destroy you, you poor fool!
Die, Gabriel Delille! Die!

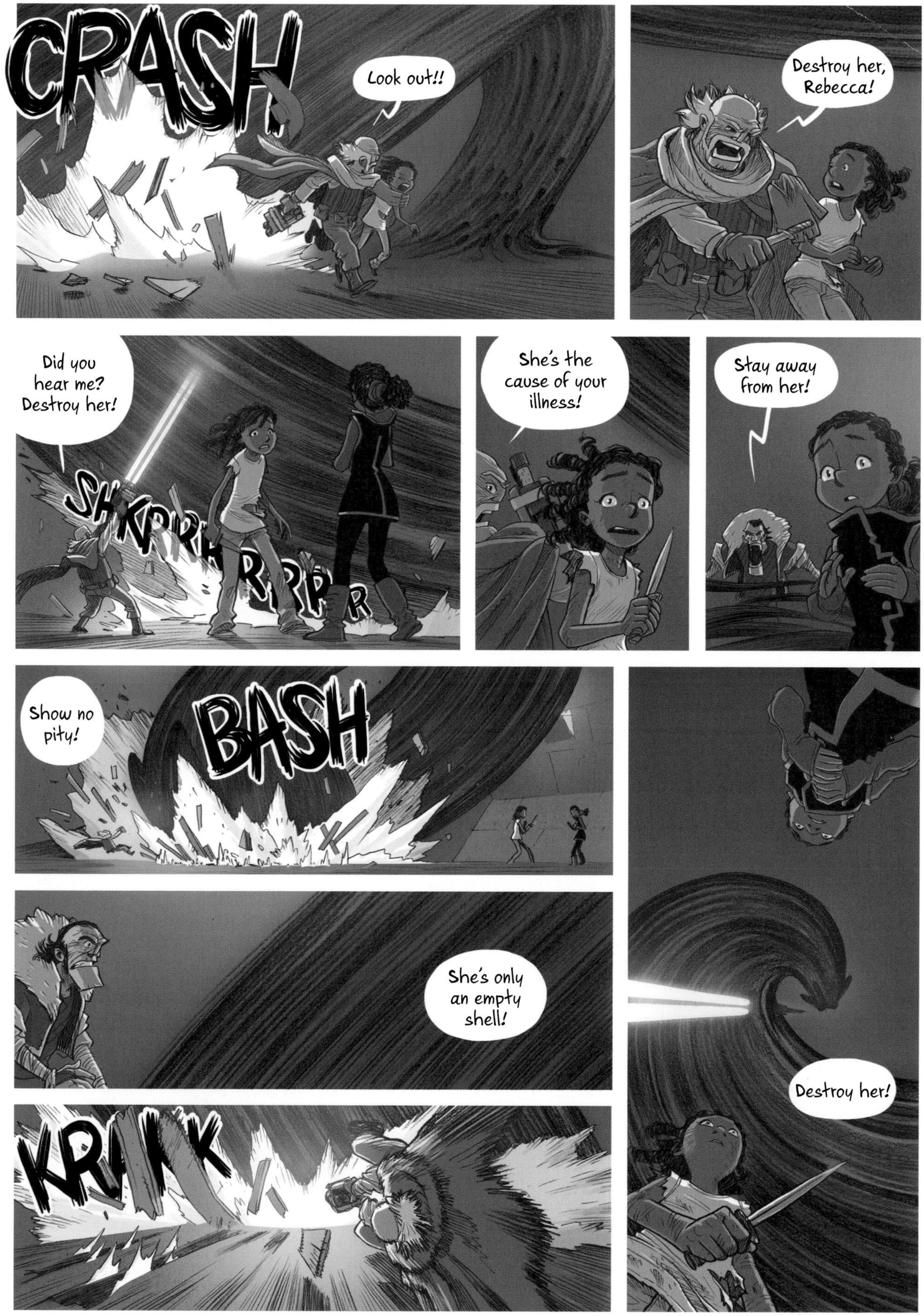

CRASH
Look out!!
Destroy her, Rebecca!
Did you hear me? Destroy her!
SHKRRRRRRPR
She's the cause of your illness!
Stay away from her!
Show no pity!
BASH
She's only an empty shell!
KRAAK
Destroy her!

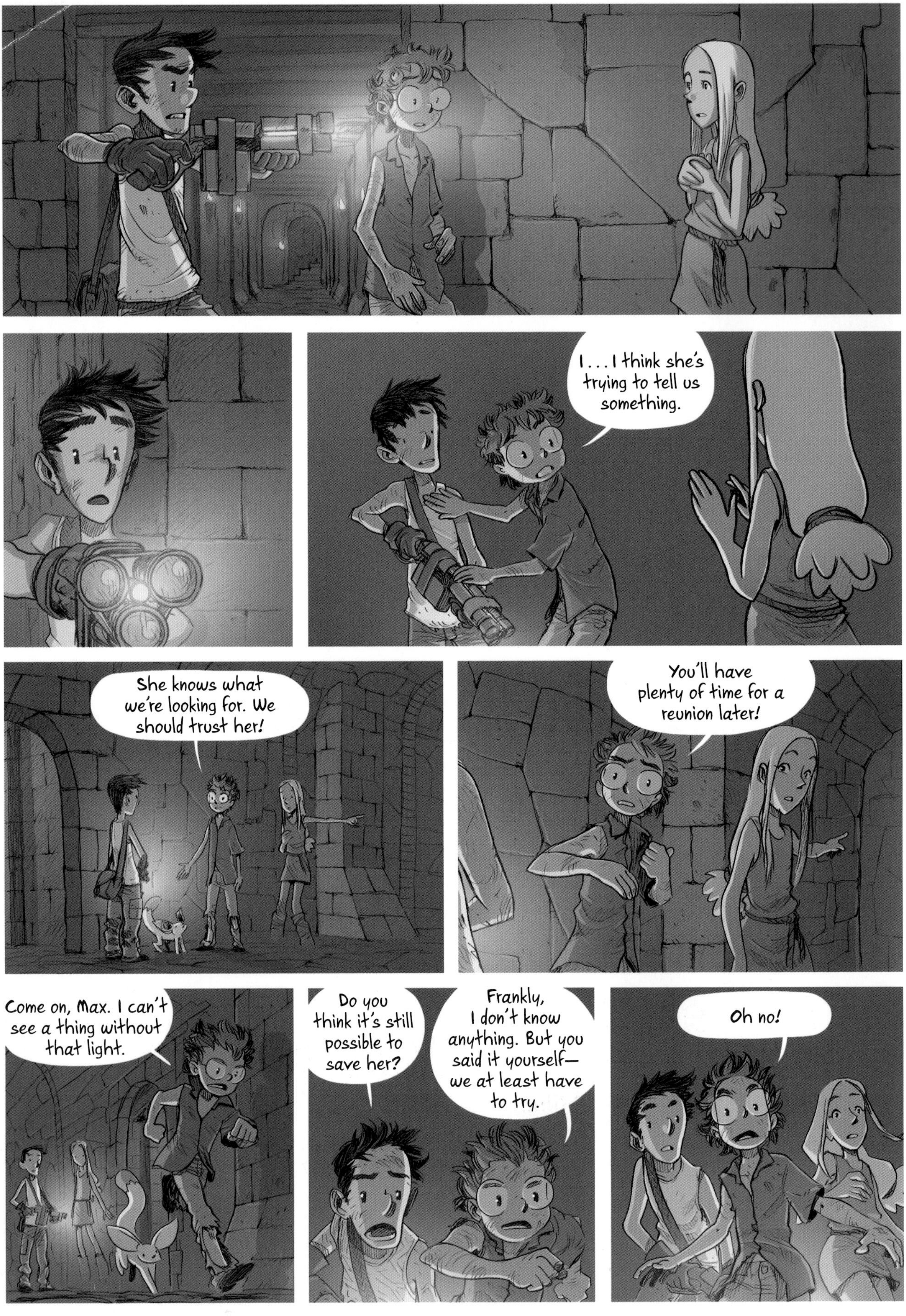
I . . . I think she's trying to tell us something.
She knows what we're looking for. We should trust her!
You'll have plenty of time for a reunion later!
Come on, Max. I can't see a thing without that light.
Do you think it's still possible to save her?
Frankly, I don't know anything. But you said it yourself— we at least have to try.
Oh no!

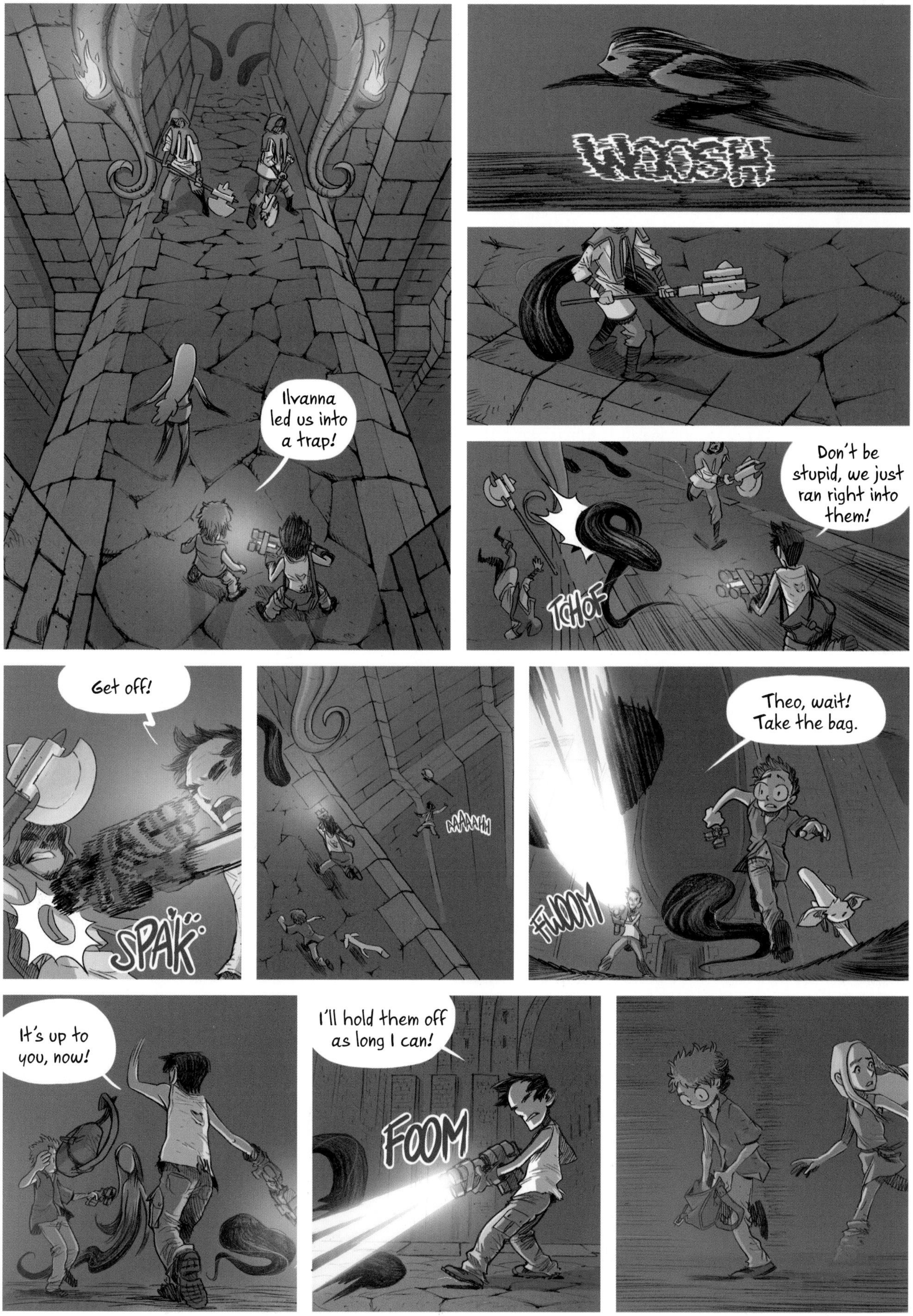
Ilvanna led us into a trap!
WOOSH
Don't be stupid, we just ran right into them!
TCHOF
Get off!
SPAK
AAAAAHH
Theo, wait! Take the bag.
FWOOM
It's up to you, now!
I'll hold them off as long I can!
FOOM

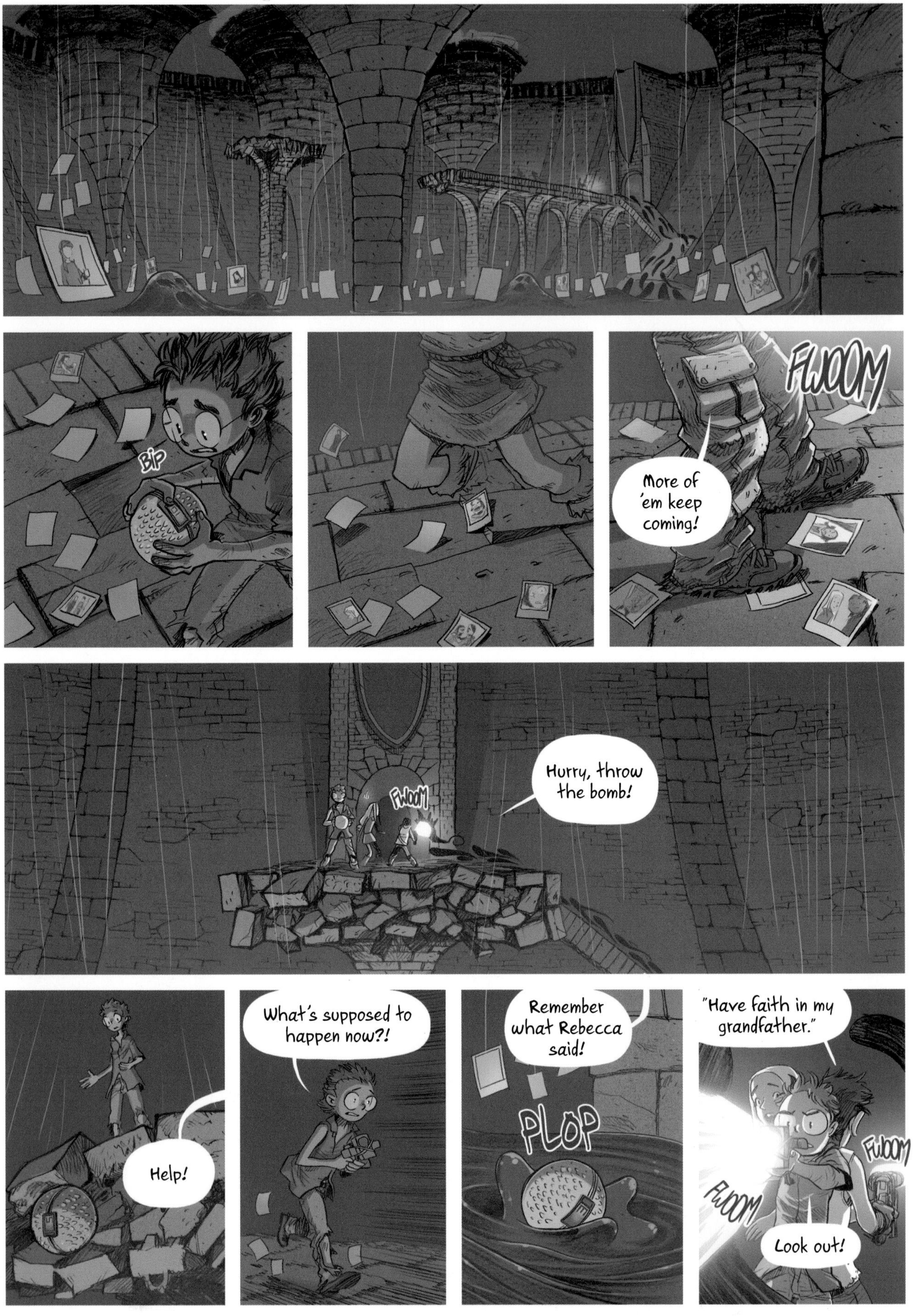
Bip
FWOOM
More of 'em keep coming!
FWOOM
Hurry, throw the bomb!
Help!
What's supposed to happen now?!
Remember what Rebecca said!
PLOP
"Have faith in my grandfather."
FWOOM
FWOOM
Look out!

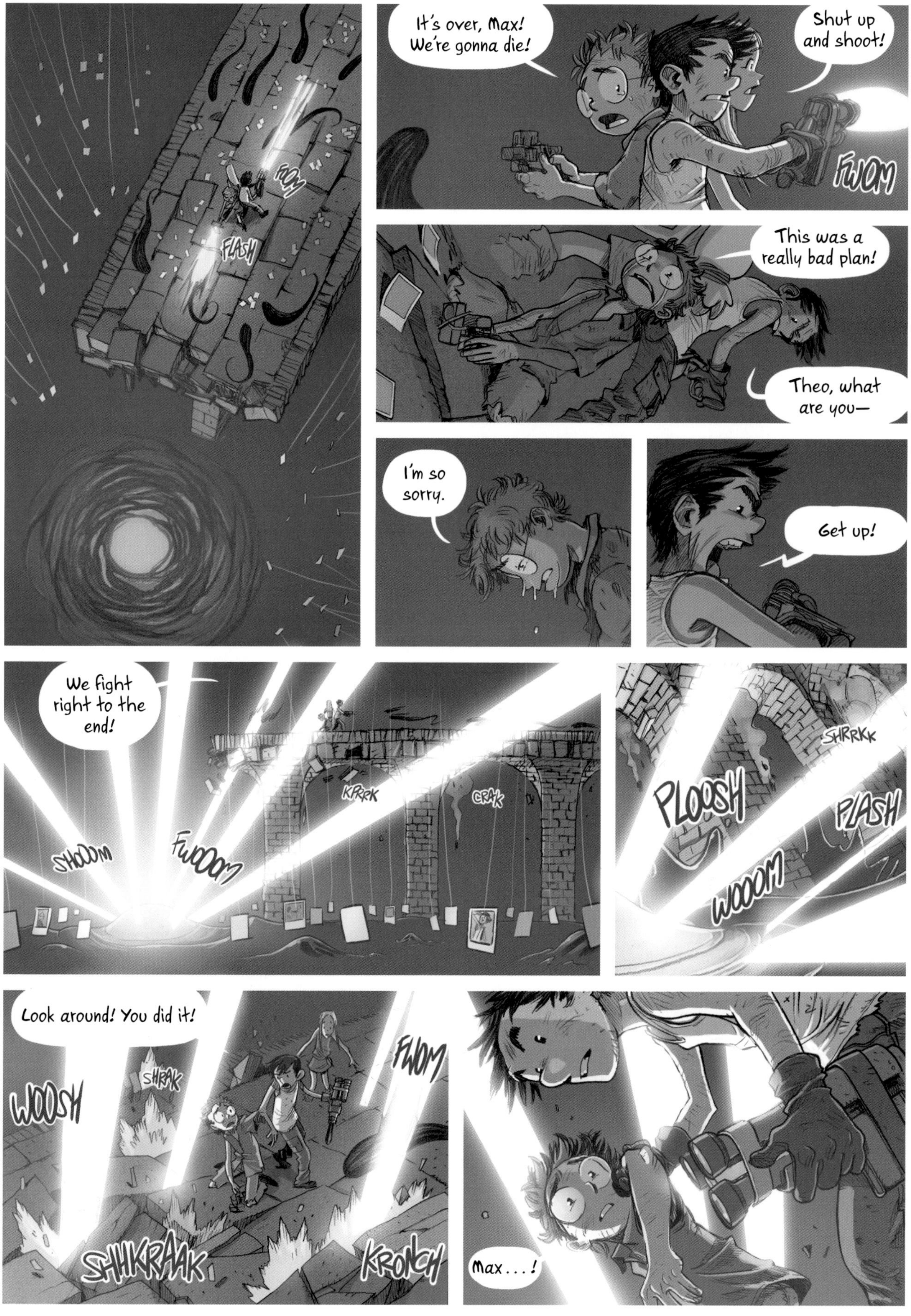
FWOM
FLASH
It's over, Max! We're gonna die!
Shut up and shoot!
FWOM
This was a really bad plan!
Theo, what are you—
I'm so sorry.
Get up!
We fight right to the end!
KPRRK
CRAK
SHOOOM
FWOOOM
SHRRKK
PLOOSH
PLASH
WOOOM
Look around! You did it!
SHRAK
WOOSH
FWOM
SHHKRAAK
KRONCH
Max...!

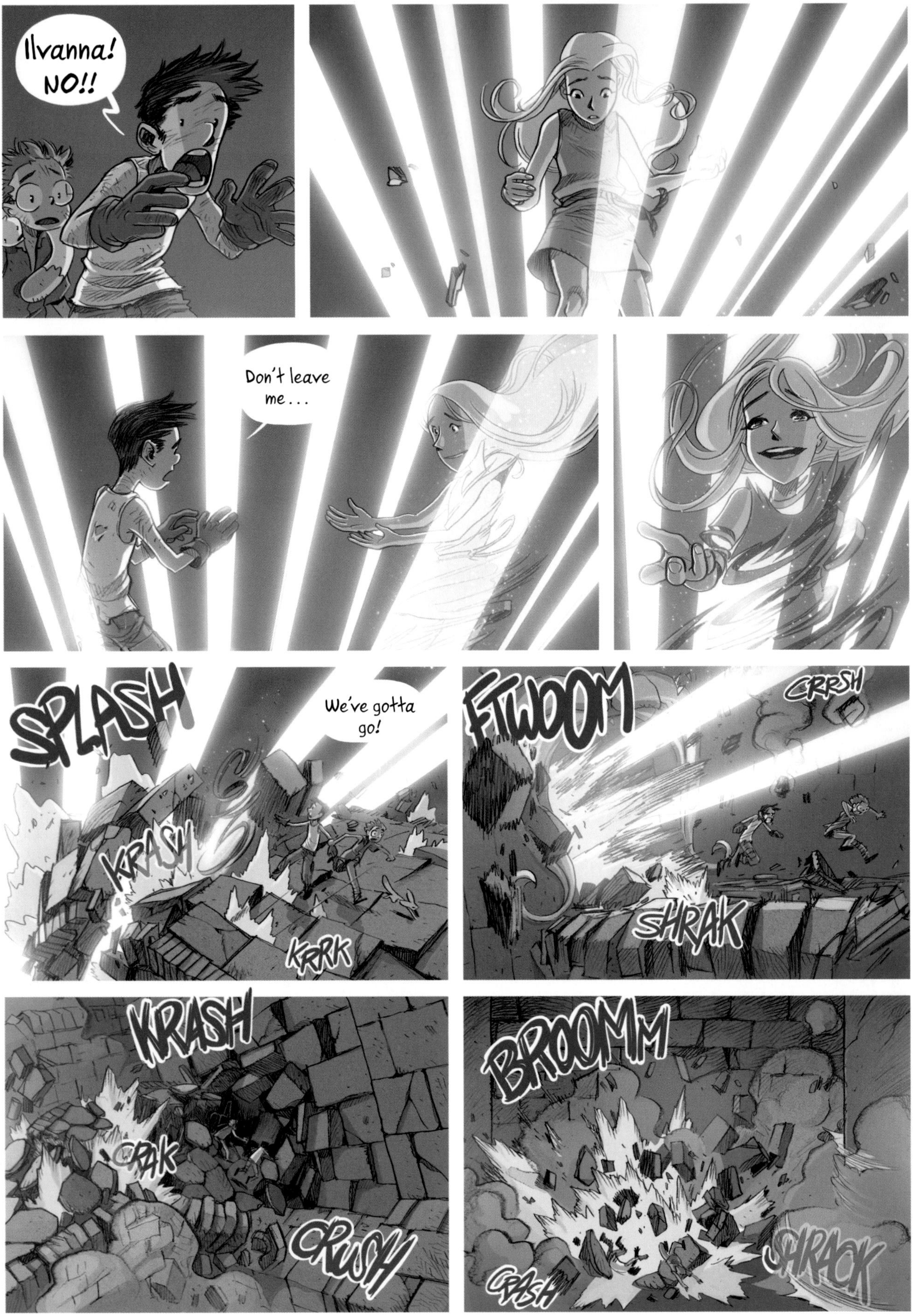
Ilvanna! NO!!
Don't leave me...
SPLASH
We've gotta go!
KRASH
KRRK
FTWOOM
CRRSH
SHRAK
KRASH
CRAK
CRUSH
BROOMM
CRASH
SHRACK

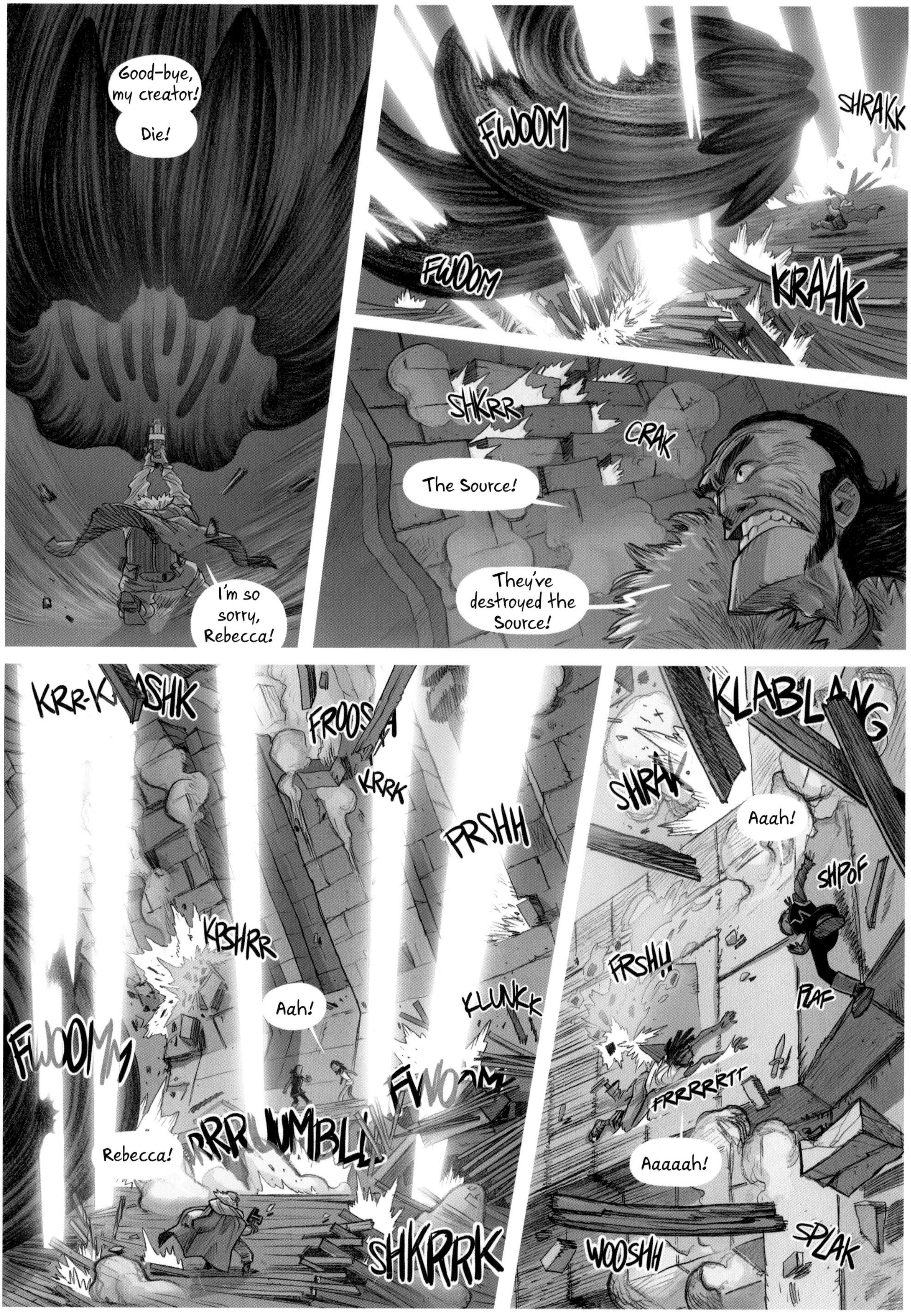
Good-bye, my creator!
Die!
I'm so sorry, Rebecca!
FWOOM
SHRAKK
FWOOM
KRAAK
SHKRR
CRAK
The Source!
They've destroyed the Source!
KRR-KRASHK
FROOSH
KRRK
PRSHH
KPSHRR
Aah!
KLUNKK
FWOOMM
FWOOM
RRRUUMBLE
Rebecca!
SHKRRK
KLABLANG
SHRAK
Aaah!
SHPOF
FRSHH
PLAF
FRRRRRTT
Aaaaah!
WOOSHH
SPLAK

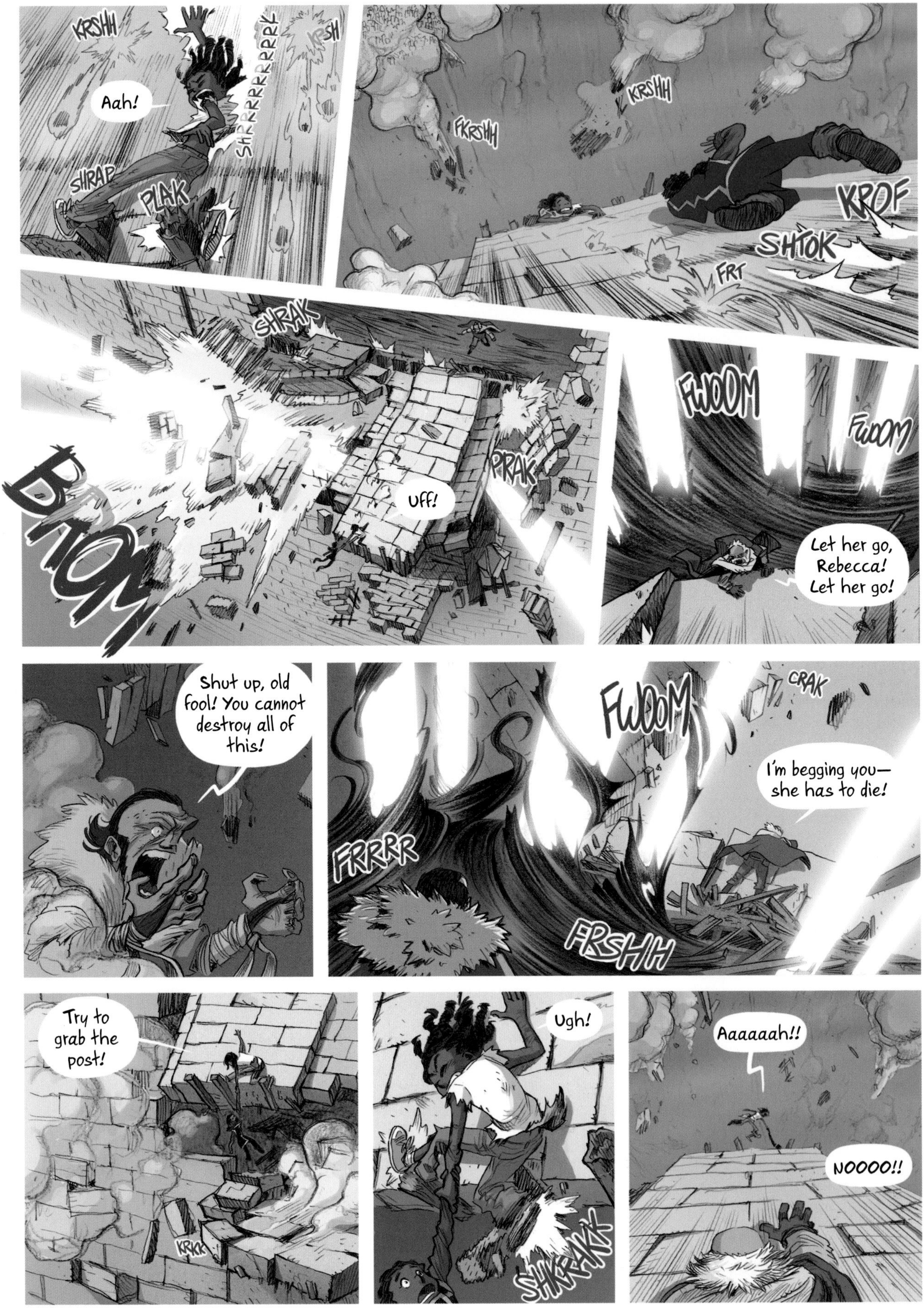
KRSHH
Aah!
SHRRRRRRRRRY
KRSH
SHRAP
PLAK
KRSHH
FKRSHH
KROF
SHTOK
FRT
SHRAK
BRAOM
PRAK
Uff!
FWOOM
FWOOM
Let her go, Rebecca! Let her go!
Shut up, old fool! You cannot destroy all of this!
FWOOM
CRAK
I'm begging you— she has to die!
FRRRR
FRSHH
Try to grab the post!
KRKK
Ugh!
SHKRAKK
Aaaaaah!!
NOOOO!!

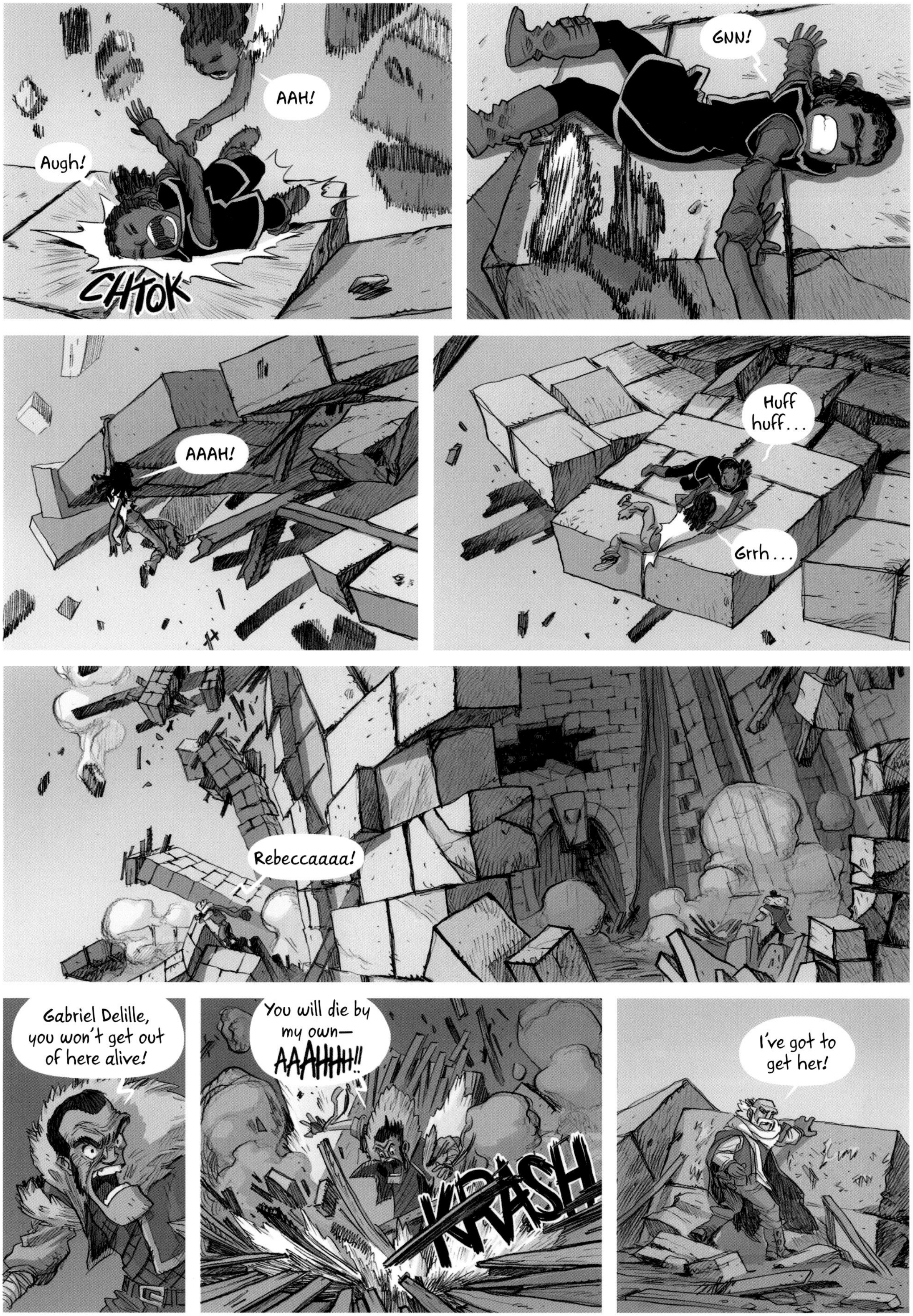
AAH!
Augh!
CHTOK
GNN!
AAAH!
Huff huff...
Grrh...
Rebeccaaaa!
Gabriel Delille, you won't get out of here alive!
You will die by my own—
AAAHHH!!
KRASH
I've got to get her!

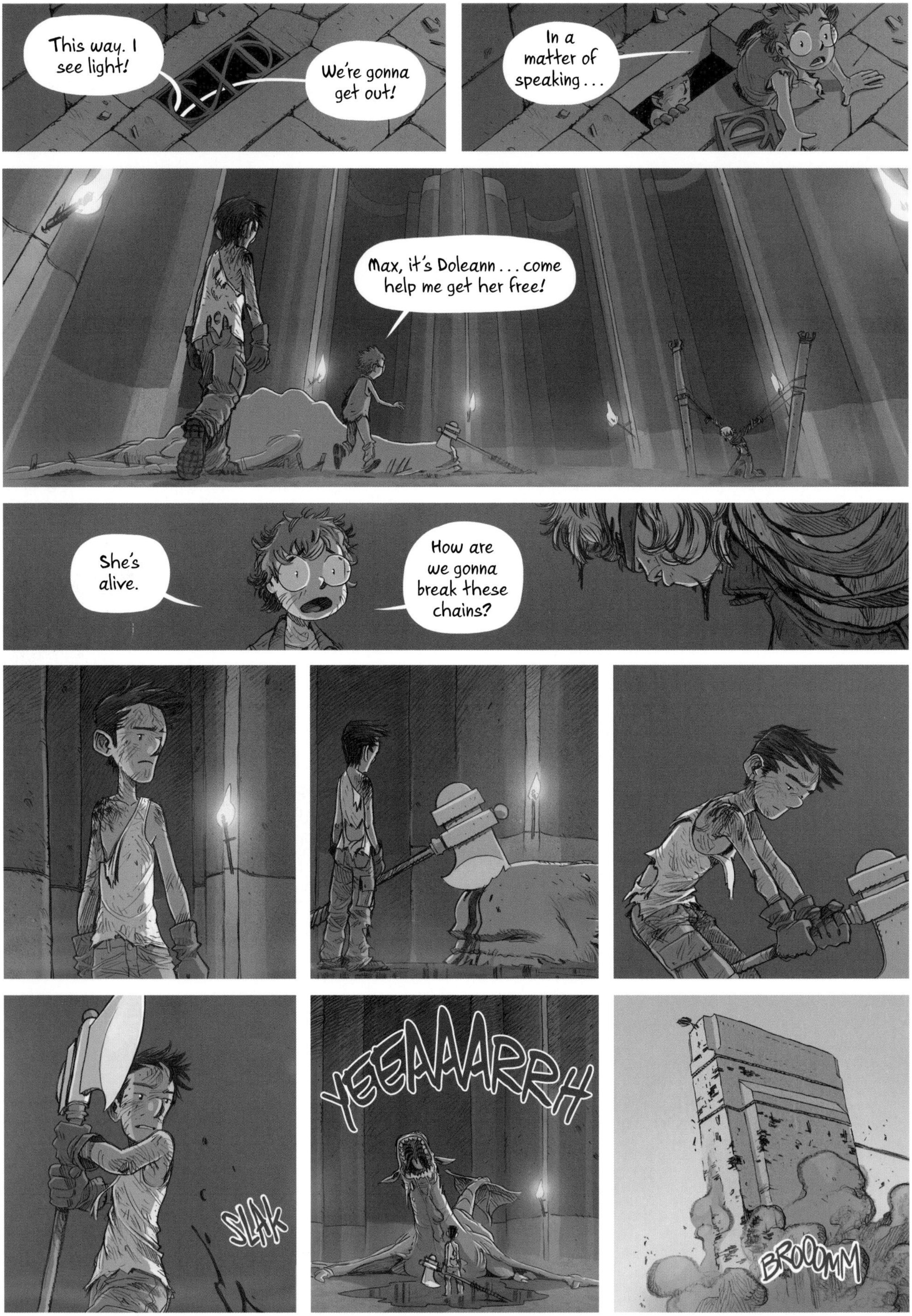
This way. I see light!
We're gonna get out!
In a matter of speaking . . .
Max, it's Doleann . . . come help me get her free!
She's alive.
How are we gonna break these chains?
SLAK
YEEAAAARRH
BROOOMM

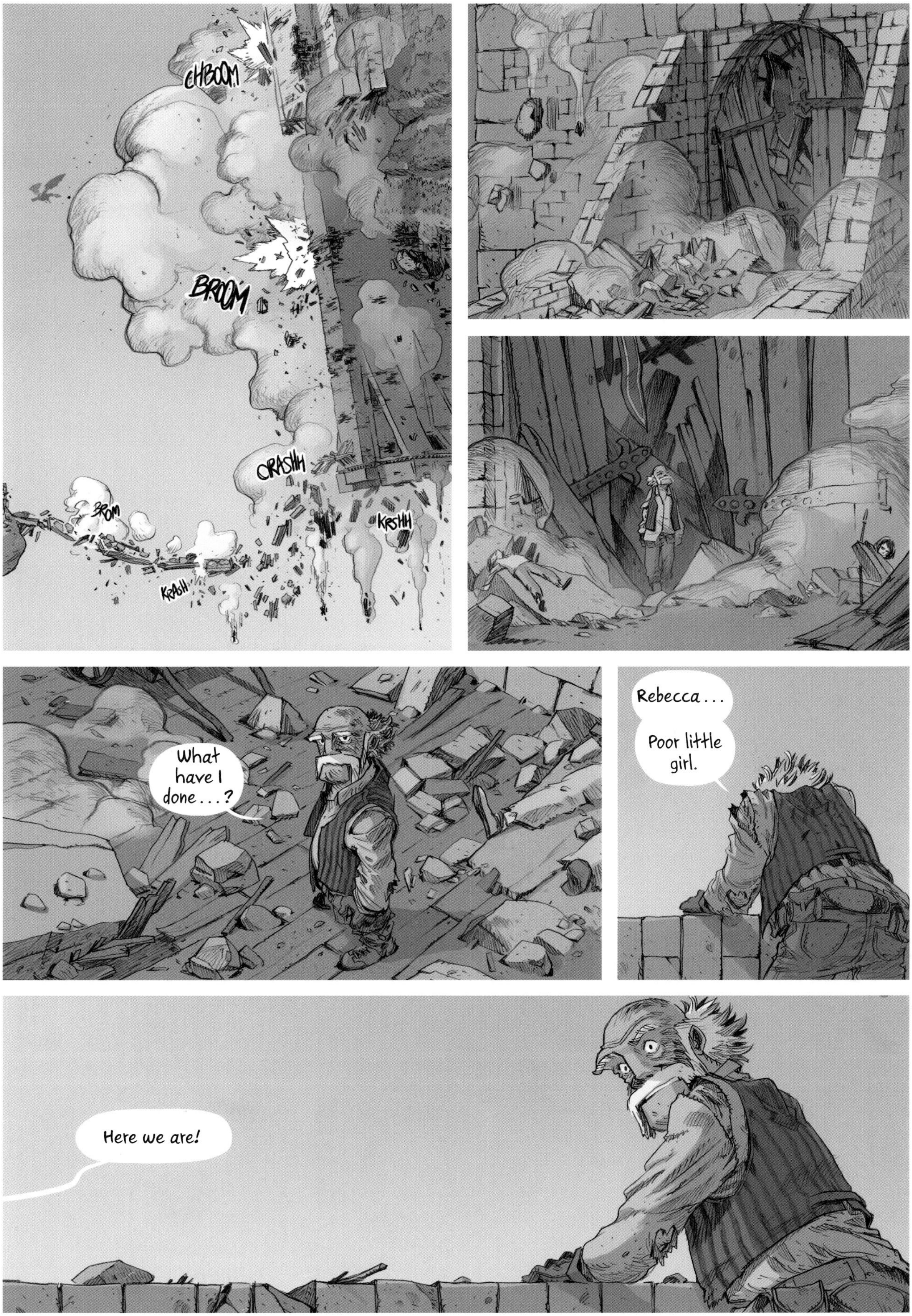
CHBOOM
BROOM
CRASHH
BROM
KRSHH
KRASH
What have I done . . . ?
Rebecca . . .
Poor little girl.
Here we are!

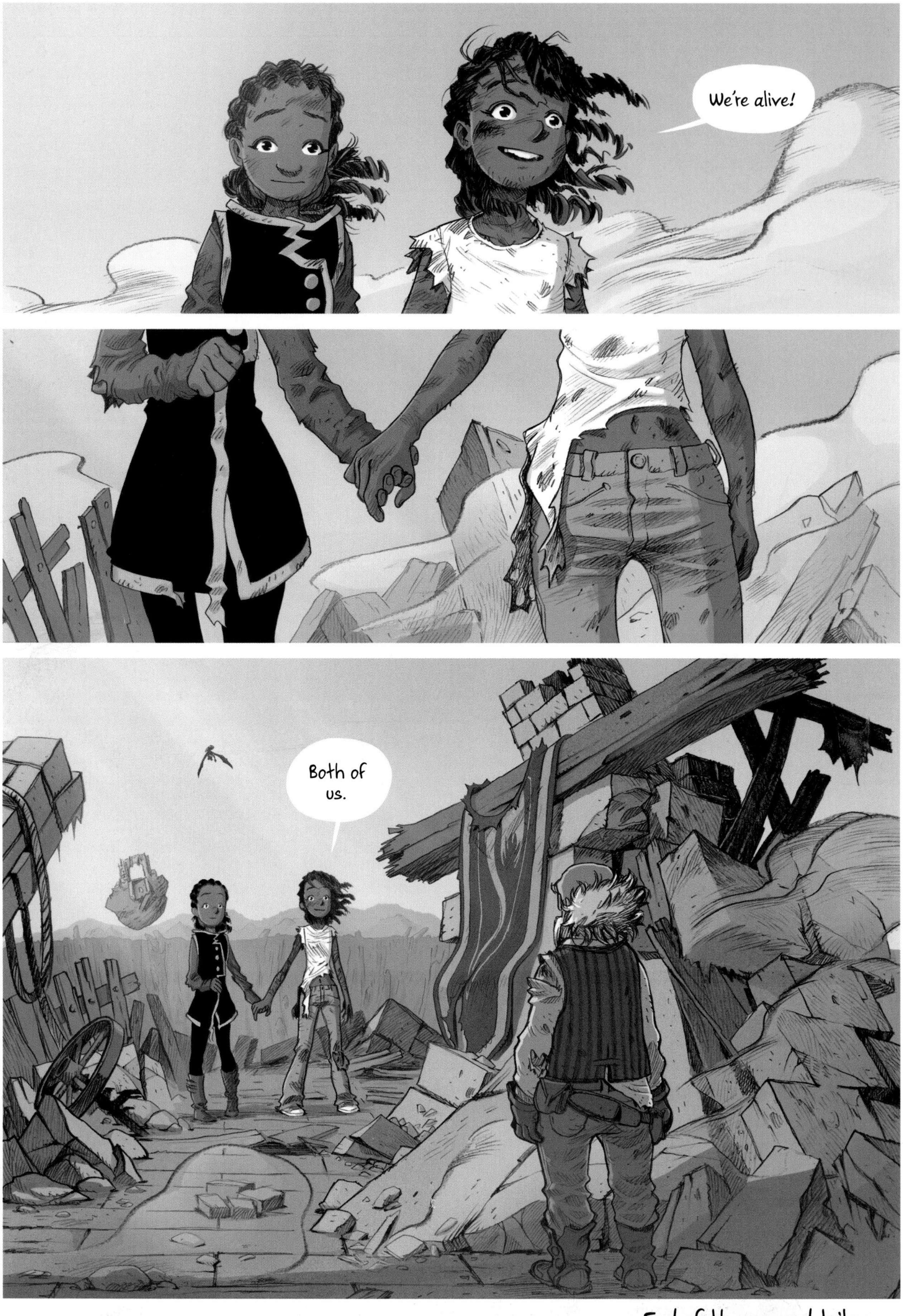
We're alive!
Both of us.

End of the second trilogy

Art by Bannister
Story by Nykko
Colors by Jaffré
Translation by Carol Klio Burrell

First American edition published in 2013 by Graphic Universe™.
Published by arrangement with Mediatoon Licensing—France.

Graphic Universe™
A division of Lerner Publishing Group, Inc.
241 First Avenue North
Minneapolis, MN 55401 U.S.A.

Website address: www.lernerbooks.com

Library of Congress Cataloging-in-Publication Data

Bannister.
[Confrontation. English]
The tower of shadows / art by Bannister ; story by Nykko ; translation by
Carol Klio Burrell. — 1st American ed.
  p.   cm. — (The ElseWhere chronicles ; book 6)
Summary: To stay alive and return home, Rebecca and her friends must
strike the Master of Shadows at the source of his powers, a crumbling
castle fiercely guarded by the Shadow Spies.
ISBN 978-1-4677-1233-0 (lib. bdg. : alk. paper)
1. Graphic novels. [1. Graphic novels. 2. Horror stories.] I. Bannister,
illustrator. II. Burrell, Carol Klio, translator. III. Title.
PZ7.7.N96To 2013
741.5'944—dc23   2013000317

Manufactured in the United States of America
2 - BP - 7/15/13

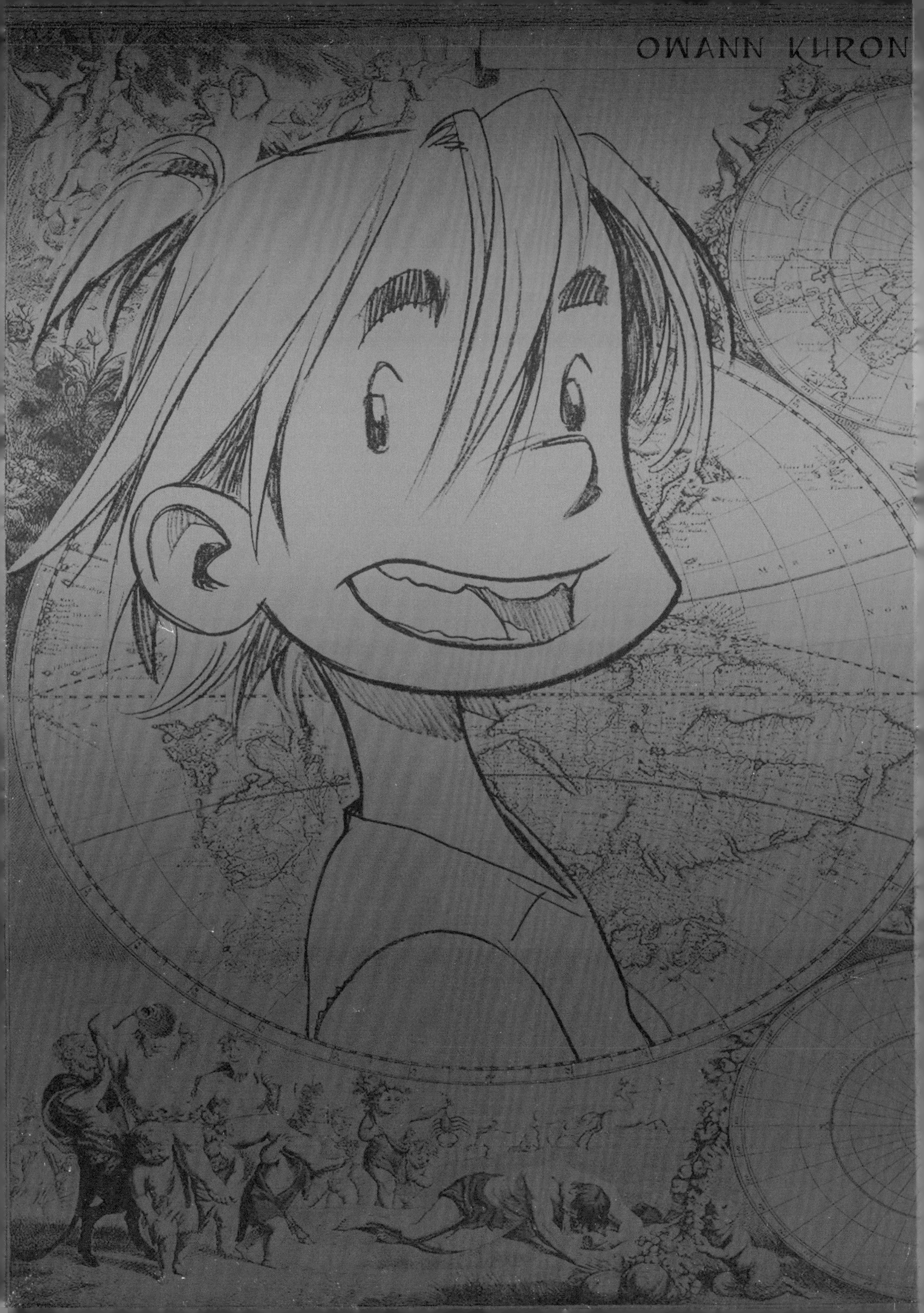
OWANN KURON